WINTER'S
PROMISE

WINTER'S PROMISE
ARC Shifters

By

Julie Trettel

Thanks and Acknowledgments

Whew! We did it. I'm not going to lie y'all this was a tough one for me. With the holidays I got behind in writing, and my editing team really stepped up helped bring this one to life. I don't have to name you all, you know who you are, and I love you to pieces!

Special thanks to Tobi Helton! You are truly a great friend and I value your input more than you know.

Chad

Chapter 1

I stared across my room to the empty bed with a sigh. It had happened again. First Chase had moved out to be with Jenna, now Damon had packed up and moved the last of his stuff out too. I didn't blame him for wanting to be with his mate, and truth was I really liked Karis. But even though Damon Rossi was gruff and sometimes rude, he was my friend and brother, and I was going to miss him.

I knew I was being a little sentimental, but growing up, my family was close, and as far as I was concerned the brothers of Delta Omega Gamma were part of my family. I preferred to have us all under one roof, but I knew that wasn't my decision to make. I was happy for them both, but the room just felt so lonely now.

I reached down to the box I kept under my bed and pulled it out to grab a bag of chips. The salty flavor I loved so much couldn't soothe me from the emptiness of my room. I had to get out of there. I was worried about winter coming; I had already steadily been gaining weight since the new school year began, and with it quickly approaching the holidays I knew I'd have my full chub back on soon.

Rolling up the bag, tossing the chips back in the box and hiding it under my bed, I grabbed my coat and left the doghouse. I thought a nice walk around the campus of my school, Archibald Reynolds College, would help clear my head and sullenness.

I hadn't started out at the ARC. My family was from Vermont, and out of high school I'd gone to a human college to stay close to home. I only lasted one semester. I was lucky to get the opportunity to attend Archibald Reynolds and I just couldn't turn it down.

My parents agreed, so they packed up my siblings and sold their home in Vermont to move the entire family across the country to be near me in California. They lived about an hour away, which was perfect for me to enjoy being near them without feeling smothered.

When I was in the first school back East, I had joined Delta Omega Gamma. They had seemed like a group of good guys, but it had turned out that they were mostly assholes. I'd rushed in late summer and was easily invited to pledge. But as the semester progressed and I started gaining weight, things began to change. The rest of my time there had been difficult and contributed to my desire to leave.

I never considered that there would be a D.O.G. chapter at the ARC, but it had been on my application and they had naturally assigned me a room at the house. Me, a squirrel shifter, living with a house full of dogs, like actual dogs. At this point every single one of my fraternity brothers were canine shifters of some sort—wolves, coyotes, jackals, and so on. It had been a shock at first, but unlike my brothers back East, these guys had accepted me with open arms. Sure, I got teased from time to time for being different, but not bullied because of it.

They had quickly become family to me, and I was very territorial of my family and my space. Maybe that was why I fit in so well. Wolves were incredibly territorial too, so we had more in common than people thought.

The brisk late Fall air was refreshing, but did little to improve my mood. Just like the additional weight I was gaining did little to stop encouraging the girls from looking my way.

It wasn't that I didn't like the attention. I had always been social, and my mother accused me of being a perpetual flirt. There was some truth to her words. I never meant anything by it, it was simply my personality.

I was just surprised they were still coming on so strong. By the time I'd left the ARC to head home for the summer, I had garnered quite the reputation. I'd be embarrassed if my mother found out that everyone on campus thought I was this huge playboy.

That had all started with Tiffany Clements. I had asked her out, and much to the surprise of many, she'd said yes. We had dated off and on for a couple weeks at the beginning of spring, but as the weight started pouring off and my toned muscles beneath began to pop out, things changed. To be honest I wasn't sure if that was a blessing or a curse. It just was what it was.

I hadn't been prepared for the overwhelming popularity that came my way. Turned out Tiffany had told everyone I was just as amazing in bed as I looked without a shirt on. Someone had captured a picture of me by the lake in May without my shirt. My winter fluff was entirely gone, and the photo circulated quickly throughout campus. That had launched me into the most popular guy on campus. It was insane.

There were a lot of species of shifters at the ARC, many of which were quite aggressive. I'd been careful to navigate the waters and rarely dated, though I hung out with many ladies on a regular basis. Tiffany wasn't the only one to start a rumor about me. Soon others had too. It was like the more I rejected them, the more they wanted it to appear I hadn't, so they told their friends that I was a fantastic one-night stand. Some of the rumors spreading of what I'd done were likely making my poor grandmother roll over in her grave, but they were all lies!

My fraternity brothers were proud of me and egged on the gossip. I was pretty sure most thought it was all true anyway. They'd be pretty shocked to find out that I was still a virgin.

As the new semester began, the tales only increased. They had grown to ridiculous proportions before they finally began to taper off some. I began gaining my winter weight and a few backed off their campaigns to find out just how real the rumors really were, but far more than that were still holding out hope that I'd pick them next. Sometimes I wished they'd all just leave me alone.

I had made my way to the large lake that the campus partially wrapped around. I stopped and picked up a rock and skipped it across the water.

"Something bothering you Chad?"

I startled and turned to see my brother, Brett. He was also president of our fraternity.

"Oh, hey Brett. Everything's fine, just needed to get out of the house for a while."

"You're starting to sound like Damon. Maybe that room is just cursed," he joked.

"Nah, I'm fine. I miss him, but it's all good. Just a little too quiet today.

"Why aren't you out on a date or something?"

I rolled my eyes at him. Brett was one of the few people who knew the truth, but that didn't mean he missed any opportunity to tease me about it.

For a while I had been dating basically a different girl every night. It was fun at first, but the excitement wore off quickly. The problem was, squirrels were dedicated creatures. I wanted a mate, just one, certainly not a new one every night.

Those girls never even took the time to get to know me. They just wanted the notoriety of having dated me and even when disappointed that I wouldn't sleep with them at the end of the night, each one swore to their friends it had happened. I didn't even understand it.

I was going to end up in a sexual harassment case if this continued. I didn't want to admit it, even to Brett, but I hadn't even kissed a girl since Tiffany. She'd been different at first, but she thought it would be funny to spread the rumors of how phenomenal I was in bed even though she did know the truth. She knew she'd taken things too far and it had largely cost us our friendship.

I was a squirrel who had been raised by loving parents. My mother had ingrained it into me that my mate was worth the wait and that I should keep myself for her and her alone. I knew that wasn't the norm, especially in college, but I believed her, and I was willing to wait. I'd seen how much happier and more settled Chase and Damon were after meeting their mates. I envied them. I wanted that for myself.

I was only a sophomore. I wasn't ready to fall in love and live happily ever after, but I sure did love the idea that it would be in my future. Maybe that was cheesy, but I didn't care. Mom had raised me on cheesy chick flicks. What could I say? I was a mama's boy through and through. I loved the time we'd spent watching all of her faves.

I'd never admit that to the guys. They'd never let me live it down.

Brett nudged me, pulling me away from my thoughts. "How about we go grab a beer over at Jack's?"

I rolled my eyes at him. "You do realize I'm still underage, right?"

"Pfft. Since when has that ever stopped you?"

I laughed because he was right.

Ember

Chapter 2

I rolled my eyes as I entered my dorm. I could hear the music pumping as I descended the stairs to the basement. I had chosen the room purposefully for its cool dark qualities that boded well for my animal spirit. My roommate had contracted mono that had led to some strange disease and had to be sent home to recover. Somehow it had wiped out her animal too, which is weird because normally the animal within would heal us quickly. It had been devastating to watch my one true friend endure all that and have to leave. It was lonely without her, but worse, Magenta moved in.

I mean, what kind of stupid name was Magenta anyway? She was gorgeous and sexy, super popular on campus, and the exact opposite of everything I stood for. We didn't agree on anything. We barely tolerated each other, and my once safe haven had been turned into party central. I had complained to the RA on our floor more times than I could count, but it didn't matter because she was friends with Magenta and had made the arrangements personally to get her friend into our dorm. I was stuck with her.

As Fall arrived and the days grew shorter and the cold began to set in, my natural instinct was to hole up in my comfort zone and just veg. But she had destroyed my comfort zone. I didn't have one any longer. I spent hours upon hours in the library just to stay away from the place. It was a living nightmare with no way out.

I should probably write a book about it, it would likely be a bestseller even. *Nightmares of Kenston Hall*; Magenta would be my starring character.

It wasn't like I was a nobody. By all rights I was one of the richest people on campus. Heck, even my dorm was named after me; I was Emmy Kenston. It was only my sophomore year and my parents had already poured in so much money to the place they'd changed the name of my hall to reflect it. Of course, anytime anyone asked me about it, I told them I was of no relation, but that wasn't true.

Alicia and Martin Kenston, those were my parents. My mother was a Hollywood diva. She had starred in more films than I could count and was currently the third highest paid actress in the world and hellbent on working her way to the top of that list. She wasn't a diva at home though. She was just mom, always there for me, a shoulder to cry on, and my best friend. Dad worked in some sort of lab as a scientist, but I didn't really know all the details. It was all very classified and hush-hush. All I knew for sure was that his income rivaled my mothers.

The thing was, my parents were human. I was adopted as an infant. They said I was found in the woods next to the highway during one of the wildfires. A couple of chipmunks, or some sort of small animals, had scurried across the road and a driver swerved to avoid killing them. When the car came to a stop, the lights were shining right on me and I was taken to the hospital immediately. It had been determined I was no more than five days old.

My parents were able to take me home two weeks later, and three months after that I was officially theirs. I never felt unloved or like I was missing something in my life. I knew I was spoiled, as they had given me absolutely everything I'd ever wanted, but I had never really wanted for much. I was obsessed with keeping things organized, even as a young child, so I never really wanted anything that I didn't have a space for.

Friends were hard. My mom didn't have a lot in her life. Acquaintances, sure; people who tried to use her friendship were a dime a dozen. In truth she had three childhood lifelong friends and had never bought into the Hollywood madness. Necessary events for her job were treated like any other assignment, all fake! She was a fantastic actress, but I was one of the rare few who truly knew the real Alicia Kenston. She was a bookworm and nerd at heart, just like me.

Unlike my mom, though, I had never acquired the talent of "fake it till I make it," as she liked to say. It just wasn't me. I kept my head down and tried not to draw too much attention to myself. People always got weird when they found out who my mom was, though there was a small, petty part of me that wanted to tell Magenta just to see the shock on her face. Things would be very different for me if that were the case. But I knew the hardships that came with being Alicia Kenston's daughter, and I had made my parents promise that shadow would not follow me to Archibald Reynolds College. I needed to do this on my own.

I had no idea there was even such a thing as an all shifter college. My dad had found the place for me, and on my first visit I knew without a doubt this was where I was supposed to be. Yes, my parents knew what I was. It didn't bother them in the least. They loved me unconditionally and if I'd ever had any doubts, they were laid to rest when I was sixteen years old.

I had gotten sick, just feeling off, or discombobulated really. Then the itching began. I swore I was having an allergic reaction to something I'd eaten, but there were no hives. My parents had a doctor come to the house and he couldn't find anything wrong with me, but I was completely miserable. I was home from school for two straight weeks. The itching turned into restlessness, and then one day, as I was pacing the floor of my room, I blinked, got a little dizzy and a hot feeling engulfed me, and then suddenly everything in my room looked a whole lot bigger.

When Mom found me, she screamed. I ran under the bed to hide. She kept calling for me, but when I would try to answer, just a squeak came out. To say I freaked out would be an understatement. I had turned into a damn chipmunk!

Mom went hysterical when she couldn't find me and called Dad to come home early. I ran out hoping he'd save me, but he started to freak too. Then suddenly I was me again, crying hysterically. Mom passed out in a perfect Hollywood diva manner, but Dad had remained calm. Too calm.

Once Mom came to and I had settled down some, he explained what I was. He already knew all about shifters. Mom did too. They were humans, but some sort of shifter activists that helped protect my kind. They said it was an honor that had been passed down from generation to generation in both their families, and that they were sworn to secrecy. The fact that they had been raising a shifter all along had come as the ultimate shock, but once they'd recovered from that, life had sort of gone back to normal, or at least a new kind of normal.

Dad was very knowledgeable about shifters of all kinds and had taught me a lot. They were nervous sending me off to an all shifter college, but felt it was for the best and I'd agreed. I'd always felt like an outsider in the human world, and a small part of me had hoped it was just because I wasn't entirely human. But nope! I was just as weird and outcasted in the shifter world as I was in the human one. Only here I was just me, not Alicia Kenston's daughter.

My head was pulsing with the start of a headache as I reached the door to my room. I didn't knock and just walked in. There were about half a dozen people crammed into the room.

"Excuse me," Magenta said before looking up. "Oh, it's you."

"Whatever," I said. I tossed my backpack onto my desk and grabbed my headphones. Plugging them into my phone I turned on an audiobook and climbed up on my loft-style bed ignoring them all.

Magenta tested me in a lot of ways, but she and her friends had only messed with my stuff one time before I'd lost it. Everything had a place in the room, at least on my side of it. She was a pig, but I'd basically drawn the invisible line in the room, and she hadn't dared to cross it again. I don't think she was used to people standing up to her. But I still let her get away with too much, like the late-night guests, the loud music, and the mess.

I was counting down the days till Christmas break, and beyond that to the end of the year, where I would hopefully never have to see or talk to her again.

It was late, and I was ready for bed. I wouldn't dare put my pajamas on with all these people here. She had no respect for me or anyone on our floor. It was ridiculous. I was still stewing over it when I drifted off to sleep.

The next morning only Magenta remained in the room. That was unusual. She more often than not had overnight guests without bothering to ask me if I was okay with it. She was still asleep. There was a part of me that wanted nothing more than to bang and slam, making as much noise as possible in the morning just to get back at her, but I was better than that and refused to stoop to her level.

I quickly showered, fixed my hair, threw on my clothes and headed off to classes. Outside in the hallway I ran into one of the girls on my floor.

"Another crazy party last night, huh?" she asked.

I rolled my eyes. I didn't know her name, but we had spoken a few times. I knew Magenta irritated her as much as she did me. "Magenta."

"Why hasn't that girl rushed a sorority or something if that's the lifestyle she wants to live?" she asked.

I shrugged. "Probably none of them would have her. Would you want to put up with that day in and day out?"

"Girl, I'm pretty sure I already do, but not to the extent you deal with it. Why haven't you reported her?"

"Oh trust me, I have. Numerous times even. But when you're good friends with the RA on this floor, well, it's my word against theirs."

"Oh hell no! We will all gladly report her too then, straight to the headmaster. Heck, I'll even start a petition today to have her evicted from Kenston Hall. She's only a sophomore and this is an upper-classman dorm."

I cringed. "I'm only a sophomore, too," I confessed.

"Really?"

I nodded. "My old roommate was a junior. She got us in here," I lied. It was true, she had been a year ahead of me, but my parents basically bought the room for us.

Kenston Hall was the dorm closest to the majority of my classes, plus it had a basement, and my dad understood the importance of that for my chipmunk. Chipmunks by nature liked to burrow down in the fall and winter months, so the dark, damp atmosphere, even with the clean white walls and extra lighting, still brought peace and comfort to me. Very few of the dorms on campus had basements, or at least not ones with dorm rooms.

The girl held her hand out to me. "Melissa. I don't think we've ever officially met."

I smiled and returned her handshake. "Ember."

"Ember? That's a super cool name."

"Thanks," I said.

"Where are you headed?" Melissa asked.

"Accounting."

"With Rodgers?" she asked.

"Yeah. I'm majoring in creative writing, but since I really want to be a writer and make a career of it, I picked up a minor in business."

"That's actually really smart. I'm majoring in business too. I don't think I've ever noticed you in class."

I grinned. "I prefer to keep a low profile."

"Not big on the attention?"

"No, definitely not."

"Probably a good thing with your roommate."

We both laughed, and Melissa fell into step beside me as we walked to class. She liked to talk, and except for her occasional questions about me, she mostly carried a one-sided conversation easily. Still, by the time we arrived at my first class of the day, I'd felt like maybe I'd made a new friend.

Chad

Chapter 3

Sometimes a beer with good friends fixes everything. Despite a mild headache from a few too many beers, life appeared back to normal the next day. It was a Sunday morning and I had a big term paper due. I'd been putting it off and knew I couldn't any longer. I'd waited too long.

I swung by the café and grabbed a large steaming cup of coffee and a pack of mixed nuts to munch on later. Then I headed for the library.

It was early so there were only a few people scattered throughout the large building. I hadn't spent a ton of time in the library, but just enough to know my way around. I was working on a history paper, and the books I needed were stored in the basement of the building. It was cold and creepy down there.

The stacks, furniture, and decoration were all a combination of dark woods and black wrought iron. There was even a classic library ladder like you'd see in a movie. The place smelled musty, but there was something else too. I couldn't identify the other smell, but it seemed to be everywhere and brought my squirrel comfort and joy. I imagined him soaring from the tallest branches. It was the same adrenalin rush coursing through my body.

I had been in that basement before and it had never felt so amazing. Mostly it had just made me cringe and get out of there as quickly as possible in the past. I could stay in that dark dingy basement all day long in complete happiness the way I was feeling.

A quick search of the room told me I was alone. I found the books I needed and settled down on a brown leather couch. The smell seemed impossibly stronger there and I smiled as I set to work on my project. It wasn't distracting, more comforting than anything else.

The day passed quickly, and I had my paper written and submitted before dinner. Still, I didn't want to leave the place that brought me such happiness. I stayed, just lying on the couch until Brett texted me. It was the most peace I'd felt in a very long time.

Brett: Where you at?
Me: Library
Brett: Why?
Me: Paper due.
Brett: Sucks
Brett: Almost done?
Me: Yeah, what's up?
Brett: Heading to dinner.
Me: Dining Hall?
Brett: Yup
Me: Meet you there.

I didn't really want to leave, but I knew I couldn't live in the library basement forever, so I packed up my stuff and headed over to the dining hall.

With food in hand I found the guys and settled into a chair next to Brett. I felt off. Something wasn't right, but I couldn't put my finger on what it was. I was distracted, couldn't focus, and I imagined my squirrel spirit was running in circles.

A straw hit my forehead.

"What?" I asked, startled.

"Earth to Chad. Man, I figure you were bound to have missed me by now and would be talking a mile a minute. You okay?" My old roommate asked me.

I shrugged honestly. The whole weird day was freaking me out. I had barely touched anything on my plate, and I suddenly realized that Damon wasn't the only one that had arrived while I was spaced out in my own head. His mate, Karis was there too, and so were Chase and Jenna. Normally I loved spending time with them, but I just didn't feel like me for once. I didn't want to make small-talk or smile.

Without a word, I got up and took my tray to the trash, and then I just left.

I spent the next hour wandering around campus lost in thought. I went out of my way to avoid contact with anyone. I couldn't determine what had me feeling so off kilter, but after a walk around the lake I decided to push it all deep down and head home. Maybe a good night's sleep would help me get out of whatever funk I found myself in.

I braced myself as I entered the doghouse, feeling an interrogation was coming, but the house was unusually quiet. Normally my brothers and I would be hanging out in the common room playing video games or goofing off on a late Sunday afternoon. I wondered where they all could be, but I was just thankful for the peace and quiet. I quickly made my way to my room before I could jinx myself.

As I opened the door, I was greeted by nearly every one of my fraternity brothers crammed into my room.

"What the hell is this? Get out of here," I told them.

"No way, dude. Something's going on with you and we're here to get to the bottom of it," Chase said.

Brett shot him a dirty look. "We're just worried about you man."

"I'm fine," I snapped.

"You don't look fine. You aren't acting fine," Chase pointed out.

I sighed and sat down hard on my bed. "I feel a little off. Probably just early signs of winter. Sometimes I get a little depressed in the cold months. I'm sure it's nothing more than that. It's perfectly normal, and I'll be fine. Maybe I'm a little quieter and introspective is all." I wasn't sure if I was trying to assure me or my brothers, but I laughed and tried to lighten the atmosphere. "You guys always say I talk too much anyway. You should be grateful right now."

That did exactly what I wanted it to, as most of the guys laughed, shot back a few smartass responses and left. Damon, Brett, and Chase weren't quite so quick to let it go. They all stayed behind, settling in for what I feared was going to be a long night.

"You disappeared without a word at lunch. You talk more than any other person I've ever met. You may have the others fooled, but I'm not buying this introspective bullshit," Damon said. "Look, we may not have roomed together long, but I know you Chad. This is not you."

I didn't know what to say or do to get them off my back. "Maybe I'm coming down with something. It's rare, but it happens. I just don't feel like being social. I'm having trouble concentrating. That's all. Humans would say my ADHD is acting up. It's nothing to worry about. I'm fine."

"Did you meet your true mate?" Brett asked.

"What? Don't be ridiculous. Of course I haven't. I haven't really met anyone new. Why would you think that?" I wondered.

Brett shrugged. "These two acted all out of sorts when they met theirs. You just have that look about you."

I laughed. "If my true mate were nearby I'd have heard her by now."

"You mean smelled her or felt her maybe," Brett clarified. "You can't just hear her and know she's the one."

"Actually, he can. You'll hear her voice in your head to confirm she's the real deal, right?" Chase asked.

I nodded. "Yes, and there's been no strange voices in my head. No mate."

Brett laughed. "Telepathy is one of the last stages of mating. Everyone knows that."

"For a wolf, or any canine breed, yes," Chase agreed. "But mating Jenna I learned quickly that other species have different mating patterns. Squirrels are very vocal and most connected to that part of them. It's one of the reasons he talks so much."

Damon laughed. "I thought he did that just to annoy the shit out of me."

I grinned back at him. "Nah, that's just an added bonus."

"See, now that's the Chad I'm looking for," Damon beamed.

"So let me get this straight," Brett said. "When you meet your true mate, you'll just be walking by and suddenly hear her voice in your head?"

I nodded. "More or less, yeah."

"That's so weird! What if you don't like her? What if she's ugly? How would you be able to keep those thoughts to yourself?"

I laughed. "I wouldn't. Plus I'm pretty sure that a true mate is designed to never feel or think those things. I mean if the stories are true and God handpicks a mate for you, then she'd be perfect for me. What would I have to complain about? Besides, squirrel shifters families are close. Sort of like wolf packs. My mom knows everyone. If my true mate were a squirrel, trust me when I say I'd already have met her by now, and since that's not the case, it doesn't matter anyway. I'm not looking for my true mate, only a compatible one. Mom would never rest for even a second if I mated outside our kind. I couldn't do that to her."

Chase huffed out his chest in indignation. "What's wrong with mating outside your kind? If she's your one true mate, you can't control what breed of shifter she is."

I knew it was a sensitive subject. Chase had gone against the norm and accepted his one true mate, Jenna. Jenna was a black panther while he was a wolf. It was an unlikely combination, but it worked for them and I was happy for them. I had no issues with that. I just didn't know how to explain to him that I wasn't strong enough to do that myself should my true mate be anything but a squirrel.

"I still have a choice, and I'm just saying I wouldn't choose that. You think Jenna's dad's bad? He's got nothing on my mother! 'Chad, you'll grow up to be a good boy and you'll mate a good girl, as long as she's a squirrel.'" I sighed. Mom would never accept anything less, and I cared too much about my family to just turn my back on them for a mate, even my one true mate.

"You say that now, but it's different when it happens to you and all you can see is her," Damon said.

Brett laughed. "My how the mighty have fallen."

Damon, and even Chase for that matter, had been some of the biggest man whores on campus from what I'd been told. I'd seen Damon in action, but Chase was already messed up with the bonding call to Jenna when I'd met him. It was hard to imagine him with ladies because he was so completely absorbed and in love with his mate.

I'd had a front row seat to watch Damon's transition though. Karis had been dating a poor kid who had decided to rush our fraternity. Tyler was on his way to becoming a brother and there were no hard feelings remaining after the truth had come out, but at the time I wasn't one hundred percent certain Damon wasn't going

22

to kill the guy. We didn't know it at the time, but Tyler constantly carried Karis's scent on him since they were close, and it drove Damon's wolf mad. Literally.

If that's what a bonding call did to a fella, I was just fine without it. At least with squirrel shifters our communication was easier. Those canines just smelled and felt their mates. They could even know she was near and not be able to find her. I prayed regularly I would never find mine, knowing I'd settle down eventually with a nice girl my mother would choose. The guys would laugh if I told them that, but they just didn't understand how it was for me.

It wasn't that my mom was super controlling or anything, she was just everything to our family and I wanted to please her. So what if I was a mama's boy? She'd packed up our family and moved across the country just to keep us close. Sure, she drove me crazy sometimes, but I loved her.

Being the oldest of thirteen children came with additional responsibilities too. I had twelve younger siblings to watch after, and that meant setting a good example. We weren't rich or anything, and there'd been times growing up when money had gotten so tight that those of us that could, lived in our fur in an old oak tree for a while. It was fine. That was a great benefit of being a shifter. We weren't out on the street, homeless. We'd had a great home, a wonderful life and we had all stayed together. That was what was important. Family meant everything to me, and I wouldn't disappoint them.

"It's just not the same for me," I finally told them. "Besides, why are we even talking about this? I'm not looking to mate or settle down anytime soon. There are far too many ladies to go around now that the both of you are off the market."

Brett laughed. "It has been nice, hasn't it?"

Damon gave him a shove.

Chase shrugged. "You can have them. I wouldn't trade my life for anything."

"Nope, me neither," Damon confirmed. "And speaking of which. I need to get home to Karis. I didn't tell her I was coming by the doghouse, and it's getting late."

"So whipped," Brett said, but there was a smile on his face, and I knew he was a little jealous of the both of them.

"Yeah, Jenna's fixing dinner tonight. You two can join us if you want," Chase offered.

I quickly declined, but Brett took him up on the offer. I was grateful when they all left. I opted for a bag of chips for dinner. I'd been eating those a lot lately and needed to remember to replenish my stash soon.

Ember

Chapter 4

Magenta seemed to be going out of her way to make me uncomfortable in my own room. My temper was beginning to flare and I knew the best thing I could do was just stay away. Because of that, I'd decided at the last minute, late Friday night to drive home for the weekend.

It had been wonderful and relaxing. Mom wanted to drive back with me and give Magenta a piece of her mind personally, but I'd managed to talk her down, reminding her it was my problem and I needed to handle it myself.

She'd probably be disappointed to know my idea of handling things was to hide out in the basement of the library until I was ready to collapse for a few hours of sleep.

I'd waited until late Sunday night to drive home. The room was surprisingly quiet, but that should have been a warning. I walked right in on my roommate having sex with her current flavor of the week. There are some things you just can never un-see. Worst, she hadn't even cared. She just looked up, smiled, and went right back at it.

I had left quickly and spent the evening out in the common room. Melissa had come by and kept me company, though, and we'd gotten a good laugh out of it. I was exhausted and happy to see

Magenta's "company" leave an hour later. I hadn't bothered to address it with her. Somehow, I was certain it would have ended up being my fault. I just changed into my pajamas and climbed into bed without a word.

Classes had been going fine. I had several projects to do, and finals would be here before I knew it. I might as well get a jump start on all of that. I grabbed a hot tea from the café and a pack of trail mix before taking sanctuary in the library.

As I descended the stairs to the historical non-fiction section that never got used—I mean, why would it? Everything was far more accessible through the internet—something felt different. My chipmunk was always aware of our surroundings and even subtle changes caused us distress. This wasn't quite distress though. She seemed agitated, but more so in an excited way.

I walked around looking for what had changed but couldn't find anything. It was such a strange feeling that I almost left. The only thing that kept me there was this feeling of comfort. I had never experienced anything like it. It was sort of addicting. I had a hard time concentrating on my school work as I lay on the old leather sofa surrounded by the odd feeling of warmth it provided.

It was so comforting to me that after a few hours of studying I simply laid down and fell asleep. The room was dark, and everything was eerily quiet when I awoke to a growling stomach. I'd fallen asleep before eating dinner. A quick glance at my watch told me it was three in the morning.

I jumped up and grabbed my books. I ran upstairs, but saw the library was already closed and had been for hours. I sighed and walked back to the basement. It wasn't my first time falling asleep in there. I'd done it enough to know the alarms on the doors would go off if I tried to leave before six when they re-opened.

Security had warned me I'd be in trouble if it happened again. I didn't know exactly what that entailed, but I'd rather not find out.

The main library across campus remained open twenty-four hours a day. It had been advised I start using that one instead. This one was smaller and mostly used by upperclassmen for specific courses, but it sat overlooking the lake and I loved it even if I did spend the majority of my time down in the basement.

Now wide awake, I snagged a book off one of the leisure reading shelves on the first floor and headed back downstairs. That feeling of comfort and warmth was still there. It made me happy as I settled back onto the sofa and opened the book. I was soon lost in a medieval world filled with dragons and princesses.

I loved an epic fairytale, and this book did not disappoint. I was so engrossed that I didn't even realize it was after eight until the alarm on my phone sounded to start my day. With a groan of frustration, I carefully hid the book on the shelf, anxious to return to it after classes, and ran back to the dorm to shower and change for the day.

Classes dragged on. I really wanted to know what happened to Elenora, and whether or not Prince Edward was able to rescue her from the terrible clutches of King Leonardo. It made focusing on the mundane subjects of math and science more grueling than usual.

The second my last class ended I ran to the café, grabbed a hot cup of tea and a bag of chips and sprinted for the library. As I ran down the stairs to the basement a strange thing happened.

"This is hysterical. Who reads this stuff?" I heard a voice say.

I slowed my approach and took a second to calm myself. It was rare anyone came down to the historical section, but it did happen on occasion. I didn't want to look like a complete freak.

Just breathe. It'll be okay, I thought to myself.

"What will be okay?" the male asked.

I hadn't realized I'd said that aloud. Taking a deep breath, I came out from the stairwell and into the room. I knew him. It was Chad from Delta Omega Gamma. He'd been the talk of campus the previous spring, and still remained a hot topic, especially with Magenta and her friends.

I looked down at the book in his hand. It was the one I'd hidden to come back to. *Great, it's bad enough the hell I'll catch if Magenta finds out I talked to him, but now he's laughing at me for reading a very good book. Can this day get any worse?* I thought.

Chad's eyes went wide with surprise. "I wasn't laughing at you," he said, and I could have sworn he blushed.

It dawned on me that I hadn't spoken those words out loud. This time I was one hundred percent certain. Chills ran up my spine. *What is going on?*

Shit, this is what it's like? I heard Chad say loud and clear, but his lips didn't move at all. I knew because I was staring right at him.

My jaw dropped open and I turned and started to run up the stairs, but my need for the end of the story overruled my fear and the need to flee. I turned back, walked quickly over, and snatched my book from his hands. Then I turned and ran back upstairs and out of the library.

"Wait!" I heard him yell after me, but I kept running.

I was safely hidden in the woods before it dawned on me that I'd just stolen a book from the library. There was no way I was going back there though. I sank down with my back to a tree and opened the book. It took me a few minutes to get swept away because I was still freaking out with what had happened back there. I felt similar emotions and distress as I had when I shifted for the first time. It was like my life had instantly changed once again, and I was back in the dark trying to figure it all out on my own.

I didn't want to think about it. I submerged myself into a whole new world as far from Archibald Reynolds College as possible and tried not to think about the incident and just immerse myself in the story.

When it was done, I felt better. I wasn't ready for the real world to come crashing back in on me. My safe haven in the library had been contaminated. My room was overthrown by Magenta, but in that moment I just couldn't care. I got up and walked back to my dorm.

Surprisingly things seemed quiet from the hall. I momentarily thought maybe someone above was really looking out for me and my psycho roommate was out for the evening. As I opened my door and heard her giggle, I knew that was not the case. I said a quick prayer that they were at least clothed this time. I'd seen far too much nakedness in that room already this year.

Taking a deep breath, I walked in. A shiver ran down my spine. Ignoring her and her guests I dropped my stuff onto my desk and walked to my dresser to pull out some sweats. I was determined to be comfortable despite Magenta's company.

As I turned to walk the short distance to the bathroom I heard her say, "Just ignore her. I do."

I stopped and took a deep breath, my hands clenched in fists. I just needed this semester to end soon. There was no way I was spending another term stuck in this room with her.

"Why?" a man said. I hadn't even paid any attention to her guests, but I turned to look. There were two of them. I didn't recognize the one that spoke. He rose and walked over to me, extending his hand. "Hey, I'm Brett."

"Hi," I said. "Ember."

"Seriously Brett, ignore her. She's a nobody."

The guy next to her stood and I gasped when he walked into my view.

Brett grinned. "Ember, this is my good friend, Chad. Chad, this is Ember."

Chad grinned at me and I wanted to crawl in a hole and die of embarrassment. "Hi," he said, looking a little unsure of himself.

I was freaking out. "I finished the stupid book. You can have it back if it's that important," I blurted out, then turned and ran into the bathroom, locking the door behind me as quick as possible.

"I told you she's weird. Just ignore her. I do," Magenta said.

I sank to the floor and dropped my head to my knees. *Please go away,* I thought.

If that's what you want, I heard him say in my head.

"Hey Brett, I think we should probably get going. Magenta thanks for letting us hang here," Chad said.

"You sure?" Brett asked.

"Yeah. It's for the best," Chad said.

Magenta tried to talk them out of leaving, but I breathed a sigh of relief when I heard the door finally close behind them. I got up, changed and left the bathroom.

"I can't believe you just did that. Do you have any idea who those guys were? You are a freak. I can't believe you scared them off like that," Magenta said.

"I'm not a freak. You're a slut. You have a boyfriend, so why do you even care? Leave me alone." I had never been so assertive with her and I saw the shock on her face. She didn't even try to give a comeback, but as I settled into bed she stormed out of the room. It was a small blessing, but I'd take it.

Chad

Chapter 5

I'd heard her before I even saw her. My mate. My one true mate. I was still in shock. The entire meeting had been so bizarre. I'd just sat there and let her leave. Replaying through everything she'd said, or thought really, the only thing of value I'd picked up was the name Magenta.

I only knew one Magenta around campus. She was a real piece of work, but I wanted to find my mate. Despite all my earlier bravado, I wanted to know her. Who was she? What was her name? Her shock told me she couldn't be a squirrel shifter. She looked like telepathy was the strangest thing in the world, and a squirrel would know that was normal. She should have recognized me as her mate, but there was nothing in her expression that gave me any hope she did.

As the shock wore off, I had headed back to the doghouse, thankful Brett was home. I'd told him everything I'd experienced, and he insisted on going with me to Magenta's. That had been awkward to say the least.

She hadn't been expecting us and squealed when she opened the door. I'd left Brett to handle the small talk while I checked the place out trying to determine if it could be the link I needed to find the girl. I couldn't get her big brown eyes out of my mind. I could get lost in those eyes.

We were just about to make an excuse to leave when the door flew open. I knew without seeing her that it was my mate. I froze. I just sat there unable to move. Brett gave me a nod of understanding and introduced himself.

Ember. What a beautiful and unique name. My mate. The possessiveness I felt towards her when Magenta told us to ignore her and called her a nobody, scared me. She wasn't a nobody, she was everything.

I bit back a grin when she freaked out and told me to take the stupid book. Did she really believe that's what I'd come for? She had sounded so sad in my mind when she asked me to leave. It was the last thing I wanted. I had a million questions for her, but I couldn't say no, so I left.

"I take it that's her?" Brett asked as we left Kenston Hall.

"Yup," I confirmed.

"She's cute," he said.

"Yup," I agreed.

"She looked a little spooked if I'm being honest."

"Yup. I thought so too." I sighed.

"Shouldn't she be thrilled and excited about finding her mate?"

I shrugged. "How the hell do I know. It's not like I've done this before."

"But you can really hear her talking inside your head?"

"Yes, Brett. I told you. I heard her before I even saw her. She's the one. Ember," I said letting her name roll off my tongue. I liked the sound of it.

"And she can hear you too?"

I laughed. "Definitely. I think it spooked her."

He gave me a strange look. "Why? If that's confirmation of a true mate for your kind, why would it scare her?"

I shrugged letting my worst fears free. "Maybe she's not a squirrel."

"Shit. I hadn't thought of that. Then what? I mean you've made no qualms about your feelings towards other shifters. But she's right there. Your one true mate. How do you walk away from that?"

"I don't know, Brett. I don't know anything right now. And I don't know if she'll even give me a chance to find out anyway."

There was the truth of it all. Would Ember even give me a chance to get to know her? I was afraid the answer was no. Everything in my being screamed to go back to that room and talk to her, but I stayed away and gave her some space. I was more than a little freaked out and needed time to process it too.

I skipped dinner, something I seemed to be doing a lot lately, and laid in bed staring at the ceiling as I replayed every second over and over. What should I have done differently? Why was she so surprised? Did she really want me to leave or was she just scared? Did I make the right decision? I still had no answers after a restless night's sleep.

Despite all my bravado and my genuine desire to please my mother, I couldn't stop the curiosity. My mate was here, and I couldn't just ignore that and walk away. I had to know more about her.

I started making a mental list of the things I did know. I knew just about every girl on campus, or so I had thought, but I definitely had never seen her before. That alone was valuable information because I knew the places I likely would not find her.

I knew where she lived and her name. Those were two big plusses. I knew she loved to read. I had seen the passion in her eyes when she'd snatched that book from my hands before running off. And I knew, without a doubt, that she was my one true mate. I'd never get another chance at this, and even if I chose not to pursue a relationship with her, I owed it to the both of us to find out what made her so special for me.

Despite years of Dad preaching to me the importance of variety and safety in changing things up, like never taking the same path at the same time to class, I was still a creature of habit. Plenty of girls around campus had caught on to that fact and used it to their advantage. I needed to change that, because one thing I knew for certain was that I would never accidentally run into Ember if I didn't.

I got up and grabbed a granola bar and a piece of fruit from the kitchen instead of going to the dining hall for breakfast. I left the house an hour earlier than usual and walked in the direction of Ember's dorm. When I got there Damon and Karis were sitting on a bench out front.

"What are you two doing here?" I walked over and asked.

Karis rolled her eyes. "Stalking your mate."

"What?"

"Trust me, it'll work. How do you think I locked down her schedule so quickly?" Damon asked pointing to Karis.

She rolled her eyes. "Yup, I'm mated to a stalker. Brett gave him a description of the girl and so far no one has left the building matching it."

"Since you're here you can confirm her when she exits," Damon said sounding far too excited and invested in this.

"He's only trying to help. So far we know her name's Ember Kenston. She, obviously, lives in Kenston Hall. Her roommate came down with some weird virus and had to take the semester off which is how she got stuck with Magenta as a roommate. Poor girl," Karis said. "She's a sophomore, and mostly keeps to herself, so talking to others in her dorm hasn't been much help. That's all we've got so far."

"You guys are insane," I said. A warmth filled me. Just knowing Damon cared enough to try to help, even if he had a warped way of going about it, meant everything to me. "Thank you."

"Are you kidding? No way are we missing a front row seat to this mating. Is she a squirrel?" he asked.

I shrugged. "I don't know, but I doubt it. She seemed way too freaked out by the whole telepathy thing."

And I'm going to continue freaking out if you don't get out of my head!

A feeling I couldn't put into words washed over me at the sound of her voice in my head. She must be close, though I had no idea how far the range on this stuff worked. I couldn't wipe the grin from my face though.

"She knows you're here, doesn't she?" Karis asked.

I shrugged, still smiling. "No idea. I don't actually know how this stuff works," I confessed.

Great! Are you saying I'm going to be stuck with you in my head forever?

Can you hear my entire conversation?

Only the parts you're thinking or saying or whatever. I don't know, but it shouldn't be happening.

Why not? I asked, curious about how she'd respond.

Because sane people do not hear other people's thoughts.

I didn't know how to respond to that, or what to think. A shifter should know all about the bonding stages and that telepathy is one regardless of whether it's first or last in the order they appear.

"She thinks she's going insane, like she has no idea what's going on with us," I told them. "What am I supposed to do with that?"

"Tell her," Karis said without hesitation.

"No way, she'll really freak out then," Damon disagreed.

"She's already freaking out. Even knowing freaked me out. Let's be real, it's a crazy time, but if she doesn't even know what's happening with you guys, then you have to tell her," Karis argued. "I'm going to be late for class. Sorry, but I have to run."

She leaned down and kissed Damon. A surge or jealousy caught me off-guard.

She turned back to me and placed a hand on my arm. "You have to explain it to her," she said.

I nodded. *But how?* I thought.

How what? Ember asked, and I could sense the curiosity in her.

We really need to talk, I thought.

I thought we were, she said. *Shit! I'm late. You distracted me,* she grumbled just as the door to her dorm flew open and she headed off in the opposite direction.

Damon smacked me on the arm three times while frantically pointing to the dark-haired girl in jeans and a T-shirt with an unbuttoned flannel shirt as a jacket flapping behind her as she ran to class. I smiled and nodded my confirmation.

He grabbed me by the arm and dragged me with him as we ran after her. I saw her walk into the English building and Damon grinned.

"Give me twenty minutes," he said before heading into the building after her.

I'm sorry, I thought, hoping Ember heard it.

Explain later, you can't talk to me during class, she scolded.

The truth was, I liked having her inside my head. Her voice brought me comfort and her frustration was cute. I even liked that she hadn't thrown herself at me. That was part of the reason I'd brought Brett along the day before. I knew Magenta would do

34

anything to get with me. She'd made it abundantly clear more than once. The other part was pure moral support—I needed it.

Ember hadn't gotten excited about our mating. I wasn't even sure she understood what was happening between us. She hadn't flirted with me or thrown herself at me. It was a refreshing change. I mean, I knew I was starting to chub up, but it had been a long crazy summer fighting off the ladies. I thought that maybe I could actually talk to Ember without worrying about what her agenda might be.

I was pacing in front of the English building when Damon came back out. He had a file in his hand and tossed it to me.

"You owe me for this," he said.

"What? I didn't even ask you to do anything. What is this?"

"That, my little friend, is your girl's class schedule for the semester. She's an English major focusing on creative writing. She's pretty good from what Kaitlyn says too."

I rolled my eyes at him. "You went to Kaitlyn?"

Kaitlyn was a Theta and sort of an adopted little sister to the D.O.G.s. She was strictly off limits and we all watched out for her. I didn't know the reason for it, I just knew I better follow their lead. I'd flirted with her a little when I first arrived at the ARC and had nearly got my head chewed off by a pack of rabid dogs. She was sweet and gorgeous, but I liked my head where it was, so I'd kept things strictly platonic ever since.

"Of course I went to Kaitlyn. What better in do we have to the English department?" Damon insisted. "So there you go. I do have classes today, so whatever you decide to do with that information is on you, bud. Talk to you later."

"Thanks Damon," I said, and he bro-hugged me before walking away.

I shoved the document into my backpack and headed off to my own class across campus. I tried not to think about Ember and focus on my classes, but it felt like a losing battle. The day dragged on and I was happy when my last professor of the day ended class a few minutes early.

I walked out to the quad and found an empty bench to sit on. I pulled out the file Damon had given me. It felt like a violation to look through her stuff and I just sat there staring at it trying to decide what to do next.

Ember? I asked through the bond we were starting.

I'm here, she replied sadly. *You've been quiet, I thought the crazy was over.*

Are you still in class?

No, I'm done for the day.

Can I come over? I think we really need to talk.

No, she said. *I have enough trouble with Magenta without adding you to it.*

I wanted to know what she meant by it. I wanted to know a thousand other things about this girl too.

How about the library? I asked.

Where we first met? I asked, needing to clarify.

I heard her snort. *We haven't really met, you know.*

Well I guess it's time we fix that.

I guess, especially if this isn't going away anytime soon.

She didn't know. I was certain of it. She had no idea we were mating. I could walk away now, and it would probably only cause us mild distress. I didn't know what to do. I put the file away without having looked at it. The more I knew about Ember, the harder it would be to turn my back on the bond. I knew the right thing to do was just leave and fight the urge to talk to her through the bond. It would fade with time and I'd never have to risk truly hurting her.

Ember

Chapter 6

I was awkwardly pacing the library. I didn't understand what was going on and I didn't like being kept in the dark. That was the only reason I was there. I knew there had to be a reason I could suddenly hear Chad talking in my head. If I thought too much about it, I knew it would freak me out again.

I checked my watch. It had been an hour since he said to meet him here. My heart sank. He wasn't coming. Of course he wasn't coming. Why would he even want to? I wasn't like Magenta or the numerous other girls I'd heard others talk about attached to his name. Chad was one of the most popular guys on campus. I'm sure he was just as freaked out by the weird, whatever it was, thing going on with us.

I sighed and sat down on the couch with a thud. I pulled a strand of hair around and twirled it in front of my face. It was just something I'd always done. It made me feel safe and hidden from the world.

He isn't coming.

"You're broadcasting your thoughts loud and clear, you know," Chad said.

I turned to see him standing in the doorway at the base of the stairs.

"You're late. I thought you weren't coming," I said honestly.

"I know. I'm sorry. I almost didn't."

"Why? You're the one who wanted to talk, remember?"

"I know, but I thought it would be better for both of us if I just stayed away."

"But you're here," I pointed out.

"I'm here."

"Why?"

He shrugged. "I don't know, Ember. Curiosity I guess."

"What's to be curious about? You can just read my mind, can't you?"

He laughed. "It doesn't work that way. I can only hear the thoughts you share with me. Mostly you've been pretty quiet. I think you're better at keeping your thoughts to yourself than I am."

I didn't understand any of what he was saying, but I didn't want to look dumb asking a bunch of questions, so I opted for a simple one. "How do you know so much about this? You don't even seem freaked out."

"Knowing about it and actually going through it are two very different things. Trust me, I'm just as freaked out as you are."

"But you do know what's going on with us, don't you?" I challenged.

"Of course I know what's happening. How come you don't?"

I stared at him like he had two heads. He made it sound like this was perfectly normal, so I just shrugged.

"How much do you know about mating?" he surprised me by asking.

I snorted when I laughed. "I'm pretty sure there's a lot more physical involved for that, not this."

The look he gave me told me I might be wrong on that assumption.

"Your parents really never talked to you about this stuff? Mating and stuff?"

I stared back at him and took a deep breath. "I was adopted," I told him. "My parents are human. It's not something I tell a lot of people."

"Shit! You really don't know what's going on then, do you?"

I pulled another piece of hair around and twirled it, trying not to make eye contact with him. I shrugged. My heart was racing, and

I was ready to run. I felt like something huge and life changing was about to hit me again.

"Okay, so um, damn. I don't even know where to begin with this. Have you even heard of a one true mate?" he asked.

I laughed. "Like soul mates or something? One person as your other half? Sure. I love a good fairytale as much as anyone."

He didn't laugh. He just stared at me. "Every shifter has one and only one true mate, Ember. Now, we can choose whether or not we accept that since we could have numerous compatible mates, but only ever one true mate. Are you following?"

"Um, sure," I said. I didn't really believe what he was saying, but I was tracking with him.

"Okay, so when a shifter finds his, or her, true mate, certain things start to happen. We call it the mating call. It draws the two together and as they spend more time together a bond is formed. Yes, we often call the physical act of sealing the bond "mating" too, but that's not what we're talking about right now."

"Fine, I'll play along. What are these certain things that start to happen?" I still wasn't buying it, but I was curious. I knew my knowledge of shifters was limited from being raised by humans, but Dad would have told me if there was any truth to what Chad was saying, unless he didn't know. My stomach rolled at the thought.

"You know there are as many types of shifters as there are animals in the world, right?"

I rolled my eyes. "I'm not a complete moron."

"I wasn't saying you were, I'm just trying to figure out how far back to go. But whatever, okay. So, different animals tend to have different traits but most of the mating signs are similar, they just come in different orders. For instance, I live with a bunch of canines. They have super smell, and they often will smell and then feel their mate's presence as their first sign. I'm a squirrel shifter, verbal communication tends to be a prominent trait." He paused, and my heart raced waiting for him to finish. "Telepathy is our first sign of mating."

My jaw dropped. I knew he was going to say it, but I still couldn't believe he did. "So, you think we're mating?" I blurted out.

"Ember, I knew even before I saw you that you are my one true mate," he said staring into my eyes.

Hearing him say my name did something to me inside. It gave me a warm, soothing feeling. My chipmunk was relaxed and happy in his presence. Could any of what he said really be true?

"You already know I can hear your thoughts, and you can hear mine. Can you hear anyone else's?"

I shrugged. "Not that I'm aware of, but until yesterday I didn't know I could hear yours either."

"Fair enough, but I guarantee you can't hear anyone else's. It's part of the mating call, and a sign that a bond is forming between us. That leaves us with two options. We either get to know each other and see where this goes, or, we walk away and do everything possible to ignore it, and stay away from each other to let the bond dissolve. It will take a while and it will leave our animals in distress, but I think it gets somewhat easier in time."

"You think? What happens if it doesn't?" I asked.

"How do I know? It's not like I've ever been through this before, and all my mated friends chose their one true mate."

A physical pain stabbed me through the chest. *Mine,* my chipmunk said. I had to take a deep breath and concentrated to keep her from springing forward.

Mine, I heard another voice. It was coming from Chad, but it wasn't exactly his voice either. I immediately recognized it as his squirrel.

"Shit, this is really happening," Chad said, and I realized for the first time that he was just as freaked out by all of this as I was.

"What exactly is happening?"

"Look, my family, especially my mother, is very adamant that I mate another squirrel shifter. I thought of course my one true mate would be a squirrel, but then Chase met Jenna. They're true mates. He's a wolf and she's a panther, and that sort of shook my world up, so I made a promise to myself that no matter what, if I met my true mate and she wasn't a squirrel, I'd walk away. I have to know Ember. Are you a squirrel shifter?"

My shoulders sagged, and I could see in his eyes that he knew what I was going to say before I said it. "No."

He closed his eyes and gritted his teeth. I felt the physical rejection and it sucked. How could someone I just met and didn't even know have such a profound effect on me?

When he opened his eyes again it was like he was staring right into my soul. "I thought I could just walk away, but now that I've met you, I'm not sure I can. The curiosity to know you is too strong, but I'm scared of what that will mean for us. You need to decide if you want out right now, before it's too late."

The pain in my chest instantly lifted. He wasn't running away.

"Chad, I don't know what to think or say or do in this situation. I need time to process what you said. I'm not even certain I fully understand it all yet," I told him honestly.

"Look, this is still very new. Even if the bond has begun, it's small and as long as we keep things strictly platonic, maybe we can keep it from growing while we try to get to know each other some," he suggested.

"Okay. If you think that will work, I think I can handle that. There's really not much to get to know about me though," I said.

He laughed. "I seriously doubt that."

An awkward silence fell between us. I was grateful when my phone rang to break it up. I looked down at the screen and saw it was my mom.

"I need to take this," I told Chad.

He nodded but made no move to leave.

"Hi Mom," I said when the call connected.

"Hey sweetheart. I only have a moment, quick break on the set but I wanted to see if you were coming home this weekend."

I rolled my eyes. "No, probably not. I'll be home Wednesday night for Thanksgiving break though."

"Okay," she said sounding disappointed. "It was so great having you home this weekend. I miss you to pieces. Can't I just come up and visit once? I'll come in disguise."

"Mom we talked about this. Even in disguise you'd be the talk of campus. Please. I need to do this on my own, but I promise I'll be home next week."

"Fine," she said dramatically. "I'll see you Wednesday. Study hard and call if you need anything. I can be there in an hour."

I laughed. "No, you can't, but thanks. I know you and Dad are always just a phone call away. Um, Mom, I need to go."

"Yeah, me too. The director is glaring."

"Well don't piss him off. Get it done and over with, so you'll be free next week. I don't want you working over the holiday break."

"Okay, back to work then. Love you."

"Love you too, Mom."

I stared at the phone for a minute fully aware that Chad was watching me.

"Yeah," I said. "My mom."

"You sound like you have a close relationship. That's your adopted Mom?" he asked.

"My only Mom. I told you, I was adopted as a baby. She's great though."

"Why don't you want her to come to campus?"

I glared at him. "I don't want to talk about that. You don't get to just know everything about me because of this mating junk."

"Okay, okay. I can see that's a sore subject. You know that just makes me even more curious, right?"

"Look, my parents are great people. I'm really close to them, but I don't want their world following me here to school."

The last thing I need is for him to find out my mother's Alicia Kenston. I'll never know if he liked me for me or because of who I am. I thought, a second too late. I saw the look on Chad's face. I'd just broadcasted right to him.

"Okay then," he said, trying to ignore it. "How about dinner? We can talk some more, but I skipped lunch, and barely ate breakfast," he confessed.

"Um, yeah, okay. I can handle dinner."

Chad

Chapter 7

I was trying to wrap my head around what I'd heard. She was Alicia Kenston's daughter? THE Alicia Kenston? Hollywood superstar? I wanted desperately to know why she didn't want anyone to know that. I'd seen how her roommate treated her and I'd already gathered that she went out of her way to stay under the radar, like she didn't want to be seen. If people knew who her mother was, everything would change for her. I fought to keep these thoughts to myself.

"Hey, do you have a car? I know a good steakhouse in town. It's quiet and more private than the dining hall. Just a thought," I said.

She sighed. "Yeah, I have a car. Come on."

We walked in silence, but just being with her was nice. She headed towards Greek Row. I wondered why she would be parked so far from her dorm. We passed right by the doghouse and Brett happened to be out on the front porch when we did.

"Hey you guys. Where are you two off to?" he yelled, and I felt obliged to stop and talk.

"Hey. You remember Ember?" I said.

He gave me a look that said, "Dude, are you an idiot, of course I remember your mate."

"We're just grabbing a bite to eat," she said.

Brett looked at me as confused as I was. He looked out over the campus and then back in the direction we were headed. He shrugged. "Okay, well, you kids have fun."

We left him still standing there looking puzzled as I continued to follow her as she wound through the houses and then veered off to the right and down a row that led to the administrators houses. She walked right up into the yard of the Dean and into his backyard. She opened a garage there and got into the driver's seat of a gorgeous, brand new, dark green jaguar. She motioned for me to get into the passenger seat. I wondered briefly if we were stealing the Dean's car, but this was Ember and she definitely didn't seem the type for that sort of trouble.

As we pulled out, she hit a button to close the garage behind us. Just as we were about to pass the house, he stepped out. I nearly pissed myself. Ember slowed the car to a stop and rolled down the window next to me. The Dean looked down and frowned then smiled when he saw Ember.

"Good evening Dean Shannahan," she said sweetly.

"Everything okay, Ember?" he asked.

"Fine, thanks for asking. This is Chad. We're just going into town for dinner."

The Dean beamed back at me. I got the feeling he worried about my mate and was happy to see her getting out and doing something normal. Did she ever? I'd never seen her at a party or anywhere around campus. Just more questions I needed answers to.

"You two have a nice evening," he said and walked away.

With the window rolled up, she pulled out on to the street.

"Holy shit, I almost pissed myself when he walked out," I blurted out.

She shot me a quizzical look. "Why?"

"That was Dean Shannahan. Why do you store your car in his garage, Ember?" I had to know.

She shrugged, and I could have sworn she blushed a little too. "It's a little much. I don't like to draw attention to myself, but my dad insisted I have this one, so Dean Shannahan lets me park it there so it's not some buzz around campus. It's a nice car, just a little lavish for a college student, don't you think?

I looked out. "This is a sweet car, but you shouldn't be embarrassed about that."

"Not embarrassed," she said as we pulled into the parking lot I had directed her to. She put in park and sat there staring out the front window. "I know I broadcasted earlier about my mom. No one here knows that, and I'd like to keep it that way. I hate that you know it. So what if my mom is Alicia Kenston? She's still just Mom to me. High School was hard enough with that shadow hanging over me. I don't want that here. I just want to be me. Sure, I only have a few friends, but I know they're genuine friends. Do you really think Magenta would treat me so horribly if she knew? No, she'd been kissing my ass with false pretenses. It's not always easy putting up with her, but I like to know where I stand with people and not the fake bravado of Hollywood."

I couldn't even imagine what that must be like for her, and my respect for her grew tenfold knowing she wasn't using her connections to benefit herself.

"I'm sort of on the opposite end of the spectrum I guess. I don't really know what it's like to have money and expensive cars at my disposal. My parents aren't rich by any means. My dad works hard to keep a roof over our heads and food on the table. It hasn't always been easy. Before moving here, those of us that could shift lived in an old oak tree in our animal forms for several months just to help lessen the burden and cost for the others. I never minded though. I come from a really big family. I'm the oldest of thirteen kids."

Her mouth hung open in surprise. "Thirteen? That's. . ." I waited for her to "insane," but she surprised me. "Awesome! I would have loved to have had siblings like that. I'm an only child. Don't get me wrong, I had a great life growing up and I adore my parents. We're very close, but I always envied others with brothers and sisters."

"It can be trying at times," I confessed.

"Oh for sure. I can't even imagine living with that many people, but how fun the holidays must be."

I laughed, thinking of the chaos I was about to descend into for Thanksgiving.

"You could come see for yourself and have Thanksgiving with us," I blurted out without thinking. It seemed so natural, and yet I had to stay on guard and not allow myself to get too connected to her.

"I promised my mom I'd be home for Thanksgiving."

"Oh, right. Probably for the best anyway."

We got out of the car and headed into the restaurant where Damon worked part time, which was why I had chosen it. The hostess recognized me immediately and led us to a quiet back corner booth without having to wait. Damon came over to take drink orders shortly after we were seated.

"What can I get you?" he asked without even looking up.

"Your most expensive wine please," I said.

He was startled by my voice and finally looked at us. He grinned and shook his head. "More like a bottle of milk for you. I'm not getting fired on your behalf, dumbass." He turned and checked out my date. "You must be Ember. I'm Damon."

Ember shot me a look of panic. *You told him? How many others know?* She asked through the bond.

I loved the feeling of having her in my head. Too much, probably. I shrugged.

"Did you tell Chase?" I asked Damon.

He laughed. "Of course I did. He had already promised Jenna dinner out tonight. You actually just missed them. He's probably on his way back to the doghouse to interrogate you right now."

Sorry, I told Ember. *It's just my brothers. Damon and Chase have already been through all this.*

"No way. Stop that mind talking shit. It creeps me out," Damon said.

"You're just jealous," I retaliated.

He grinned. "Karis knows all I think about is sex. She doesn't need to hear my thoughts on a constant basis. I already show her with my actions." He waggled his eyebrows and Ember burst out laughing.

I smacked Damon, "Just get us a couple drinks."

"What will the lovely lady have?" he asked.

"Just a Coke is fine," she said.

"Same," I said.

He stopped and shot me a look. All the brothers knew that caffeine hyped me up, but I felt like I needed the extra boost to sort through all the crazy stuff going on anyway.

He left us, and I quickly apologized for his actions.

"It's fine," she assured me. "I told you, I like to know where I truly stand with people, and he doesn't seem like the type to hold much back."

I laughed. "You could definitely say that."

Damon returned with a Coke for Ember and a Sprite for me. "Sorry, only enough for one Coke."

"Asshole."

"You can thank me later. Are you guys in a rush?" he asked.

"No," I said.

"Great, 'cause I got a few other tables to attend. I'll get back around for dinner orders soon." To Ember he nodded. "Just give a wave when you're ready to order. Take as long as you need."

She eyeballed my drink and I sighed. "Caffeine makes me really hyper so as a rule I tend to avoid it."

"Then why did you order a Coke?" she asked, laughing.

I shrugged. I didn't have an answer for that, but I loved the sound of her laughter and hoped to hear it more often.

There wasn't any of the tension and nervous energy I expected on a first date. I felt more comfortable with Ember than I'd ever felt with anyone. She had said she liked genuine people, and I vowed to let my guard down and just be me. She'd either like it or she wouldn't.

I took a moment to really look at her. She had gorgeous almond shaped brown eyes, but she often pulled her hair in front of her face making it hard to see them. Her hair was dark, wavy, and I would imagine most girls would have tried to either straighten or fully curl it, but I loved the sort of wild natural appeal of it.

She could have had the top of the line best clothes on the market if she wanted, yet she chose basic jeans and a T-shirt and had a flannel shirt either open like a jacket or tied around her waist as it was now. I was having a hard time combining the girl before me with the daughter of Alicia Kenston who drove a high-end luxury car yet hid both facts from everyone.

Altogether she was proving to be a giant puzzle I desperately needed to solve. I was fascinated by her.

We discussed all the basic stuff first—favorite color, favorite foods, favorite everything. I learned she was an English major focusing in creative writing and minoring in business. Okay, so I already knew that from Damon and Karis's snooping, but I liked that she shared it with me too.

"Kenston Hall was recently renamed. Is it after your family?" I asked, just out of curiosity.

She immediately shook her head no, then stopped and sighed. "Yes, my dad made a very sizable donation and the Dean insisted, but no one needs to know that either. I always tell people no, that it's just a weird coincidence."

I looked at her, frustrated. "You say you like genuine people, yet you hide who you are from everyone. I don't get it."

"I don't expect you to understand, and I can't really explain it, Chad. People change. Even friends treat me different when they find out who my parents are and where I come from. I'm not like the rest of you. I wasn't raised in a shifter family. I didn't know such a thing existed until it happened to me three years ago. My whole world changed the day I first shifted, and I'm still trying to wrap my head around it all. I don't even fully know who I am," she confessed, and I knew instantly she was completely sincere.

"I hadn't thought about that. I mean you said you were adopted and raised by humans, but I didn't stop to think of what that meant for you. Is that the real reason why you don't want your parents to come here? They don't know about you, do they?"

She bit her bottom lip and pulled a strand of hair to cover her face from me as she twirled it. I'd noticed her doing that a lot, like she was hiding from the world.

"My parents know," she said softly.

I took a deep breath and nodded. Humans weren't supposed to know about our kind.

"I know that," she confessed. Obviously I'd broadcasted that thought to her. "Somehow they already knew though. I would have lost my mind if I hadn't had my dad to talk to about everything. Though clearly he doesn't know as much as he thinks, or he would have warned me about this mating stuff."

She blushed, and it was cute. I held back my desire to reach out and take her hand.

"How old were you the first time you shifted?" I asked.

"Sixteen," she confessed.

"Wow, that's young. I was seventeen, but I have a brother and sister who are twins, as well as another sister just a year younger than me, and they all shifted shortly after I did. I think it was out of necessity. That's when we moved into the oak tree to be less of a burden and support the younger kids. The twins were barely fifteen," I confessed. "And no, that's not something I readily admit to people either."

There was so much more to Ember than I first realized. The more I got to know her, the more I liked her. Why couldn't she just be a squirrel? I'd take her right then and there and complete this bond if that were the case. But since it wasn't, I knew I needed to walk away, as getting to know her was only going to make it that much harder.

She looked at her watch. "Wow, we've been here over an hour already. Why hasn't your friend come back yet?"

I grinned. "I did pick this place for a reason. I knew he'd leave us alone to talk. If you're ready to order, just give him a wave. I promise he's been watching us all night."

"Do you know what you want? You haven't even looked at the menu."

I laughed. "I knew what I wanted before we got here. Do you need a minute to look over the menu?"

She shook her head. "Are you going to be offended if I order salad? I know this is a really nice restaurant, but honestly, I don't eat a lot of meat. I'm not a total vegetarian, but close."

"Why would that offend me?"

"Well, it's a steakhouse," she said like that should mean something to me.

I laughed. "I only came because I knew Damon would leave us alone to talk without trying to rush us out the door. The strawberry pecan salad is amazing. It's what I always get."

"Oh," she said, and I could see her relax some. "That's what I was looking at."

"Perfect," I said, not knowing if I was referring to the salad or the girl. I shook it off and waved Damon over.

"Refills or ready to order?" he asked.

"Both. Two. . ."

"Strawberry pecan salads," he finished.

"You really do order that every time?"

"I told you I do." I grinned at her.

"Okay, be right out, but no rush. I'm working till ten, so you got all evening. If this guy starts to bore you, just wave and I'll come to the rescue," Damon told Ember.

I shoved him away, and he laughed.

"I've pretty much stayed away from the Greek scene here, but Brett and Damon both seem pretty cool," she said.

"Don't like parties?" I asked.

She shrugged. "Some I do. Some I don't. Just depends on the party. I think I spent too much time in early high school at them. Shifting for the first time changed me. I still forced myself to go because it was sort of expected, but I felt like an outsider, a fraud after that. The weirdo amidst all the humans. Here it isn't expected. Actually, my roommate would probably freak out if I showed up at a party, especially one at the doghouse. No offense, it's just she'd do just about anything to get in with you guys."

I rolled my eyes. "I'm well aware of Magenta, and I try to steer as far away from her as possible.'

"If you know that then why on earth did you come by our room yesterday?"

"Simple, because you had thought her name and it was the only lead I had to find you," I said. "I wasn't dumb enough to go alone, though."

We were both laughing when Damon brought over the salads.

He smiled. "It's really good to see you back to normal, my little chatterbox friend."

I shoved him again and told him to get lost, but he just brushed it off and grabbed a chair to pull up to the end of our table, then sat down and joined us.

"So, Ember, that's a unique name. What's the story behind it?" he asked. I shot him a weird look. I hadn't even considered there might be something to her name.

"There is actually. A few days after my birth, or so they guessed, a massive wildfire struck the area. They say some small animals ran out into the street and a car swerved to avoid them. He spun out and when he came to a stop, the lights were shining bright on me, a tiny newborn bundled in a blanket surrounded by a raging fire. He snatched me up and once they were to safety dropped me off at the nearest hospital. My parents adopted me a few days later, and named me Ember because, well, fire."

"That's cool. And seriously what are the odds that a shifter couple would be around to adopt you?"

"Not very high," I said. "Her parents are human."

Ember shot me a wary look, but I knew Damon would handle the information well.

"Oh shit. You must have been quite the surprise when you shifted for the first time. You are a shifter, right?"

She laughed. "I am, and it was, but I've handled it as best I can and so have they."

Damon gave me a worried look. "Your parents know what you are?"

Ember laughed. "That's not exactly something easy to hide, especially when I had no idea what was happening to me."

"How'd you get around that?"

She hesitated. *People aren't supposed to know my father already knew about our kind. It's as much a secret as we are.*

"Her dad's a scientist and had heard about shifters. Most find it bunk but there are some that believe. She sort of debunked that theory for him and he helped her through it," I lied, having no idea what her father did.

"Scientists. You're all nothing but trouble," Damon said with a frown on his face.

"I take it you're a science major?" Ember said, amused.

I nodded and smiled. *Sorry, it was the first thing that popped into my head.*

And eerily accurate, she said through the bond.

"Stop that. Chase is always complaining about Kelsey and Kyle doing that shit. Now I know how annoying it can be," Damon complained. He looked down at his watch. "I only had a ten-minute break, so need to get back to work, but Ember, it was really nice to meet you. Chase and I are having the brothers over this weekend. Our mates will be there. I'm sure Karis will be thrilled to meet you. Chad's required to come, and you should come with him."

I kicked Damon under the table. Platonic, strictly platonic, I reminded myself. I wasn't ready to incorporate her into my entire life, though my squirrel seriously disagreed. *Mate,* he insisted.

"Maybe," Ember said. "But thanks for the invite."

Ember

Chapter 8

Dinner had been fantastic. Chad was right about that salad. I could get very addicted to that place. I knew Mom and Dad would love it too.

I laid in bed staring at the ceiling. Magenta was gone when I got home, thank God! I had so much to process my head was spinning. Chad was actually a really cool guy. He was nice, and I felt like he was genuine. I feel like I would know if he had lied to me, maybe it had something to do with the bond.

I loved to read stories about soulmates, but I'd never believed in them. Overall, Chad seemed absolutely perfect, and I very much wanted to believe in this "one true mate" concept he told me about, but I still hesitated. It just all felt a little too perfect.

Sure, I wasn't a squirrel, but I was a chipmunk and that was pretty dang close, wasn't it? I needed to talk to Dad and find out what he knew about this stuff. I didn't really know who else to ask.

There was a soft knock at my door and I begrudgingly got up to answer it, surprised to find my friend Melissa there.

"Hey, what's up?" I asked.

"It sounded quiet for once, so I thought I'd take a chance you were here. I was hoping we could go get some coffee or something, but I see you're already in your PJ's," she said, sounding disappointed.

"Yeah, but I can change. Or if you like tea, I could make us some hot tea and we could hang out here. I don't often have this room to myself."

She rolled her eyes. The entire floor was aware of that fact.

"Where is the evil witch?" she asked, accepting my offer and coming inside.

I quickly got to work on heating up some water in my electric kettle.

"Don't know, really don't care. I'm just happy she's not here," I confessed.

When the water was ready, I poured two cups and steeped the tea before handing one to Melissa and settling down next to her on the couch.

"So, what's new with you?" I asked her.

"Not much. My roommate is driving me crazy, but that's not really anything new."

"How so this time?"

"It looks like she has a new boyfriend. It's all she talks about. She swears he's the one, but he's not her true mate. I guess I'm just old-fashioned or something. I still believe in true mates, and I'm going to wait for my one and only."

I nearly choked on my tea. Until today I had never even heard the term.

"Tell me about true mates. What's the big deal with it?" I asked, trying to sound casual.

"Seriously? It's just like, well, everything. I mean God handpicked one special person for each of us, or at least that's how my grandmother tells the story. One person, one perfect match, one true mate. It's so romantic. I know not everyone is lucky enough to find theirs, I mean, it's a really big world. But I just have to believe mine's out there waiting for me too, and I cannot wait to meet him." She nearly squealed with excitement just talking about it.

"What if he doesn't want you? What if he doesn't like you? Or what if you don't like him?" I asked.

She scrunched up her nose at me. "I don't think that's how it works for true mates. I mean, sure you still have a say in whether we choose to accept him or not, but why wouldn't you? He may not be perfect, but he's perfect for you," she insisted.

"But how will you know that's true?"

"You'll just know. You'll feel it. Grandmother says that when you first feel his presence it gives you goosebumps. And when you meet, face-to-face, the rest of the world just sort of falls away until all you can see is him." She sounded so dreamy, I wanted to believe her.

"Doesn't the whole hearing him inside your head part freak you out a little?" I asked.

"Oh, that comes later. I would hate it if that were the first step. Like what if you didn't even know the guy and you suddenly started hearing everything he thought?" She shook her head. "No way."

I sagged back into the couch. "Well, that's apparently the first sign for my kind," I confessed.

Melissa stared at me for a moment. "I'm so sorry, Ember. I didn't know."

I shrugged. "I guess it all ends up the same in the end."

She gave me a weird look and I felt like she was seeing right through me. "Have you met your one true mate, Ember?"

Was I really that transparent? I didn't want to admit it because Chad had already made it clear he wasn't going to bond with me—whatever that meant—since I wasn't a squirrel, but everything was so overwhelming that I needed a friend to talk to about it. It couldn't be a coincidence that Melissa had brought up this subject now, right?

"Am I really that transparent?" I asked her.

Her eyes went wide. "Oh my gosh! Are you serious? When? Where? Who?"

"Shhh," I warned her. "I don't want anyone to know. Please," I practically begged. "You just brought it up, and I could really use a friend right now. Honestly, I'd never even heard the term "one true mate" before today. He had to explain it all to me, and it was really embarrassing," I confessed.

"It happened today?" she asked.

"Yesterday actually, but I didn't know what was happening and sort of freaked out." I hid my face behind one of the throw pillows on the couch and regretted saying anything.

"Hey, it's okay. Everything's going to be just fine," she assured me. "What's he like?" she asked curiously.

I shrugged again. "He's actually really sweet. He's easy to talk to. We went to a restaurant off campus tonight for dinner just to talk and get to know each other. The more we talked the more I liked him, but I don't want to like him. I'm pretty sure he's going to break the bond anyway, so what's the point? And what does that even mean?"

She frowned, and her forehead crinkled. "He told you he's going to break the bond?"

I shrugged. "He asked if I was a squirrel shifter and I said no. Then something about how his mother would never accept anyone that wasn't a squirrel, so it wasn't really possible. I don't know."

"He's a squirrel shifter?" Melissa asked.

I nodded.

"Girl, they can be hot, like super sexy hot. But you're a chipmunk. Isn't that close enough?"

"Apparently not. It's squirrel or nothing, so I don't even know why he's wasting time trying to get to know me. Won't it just hurt more in the long run? That's how he made it sound at least."

"If your bond grows, then yes. Chances are he can't just walk away from you Ember. Think of it like the universe is trying to pull the two of you together and the more you try to resist, the harder it becomes."

"So what? I shouldn't resist it? I should just accept that this guy I had never spoken to before yesterday is the one I'm just destined to spend my life with?"

"Yes," she said, giving no room for argument. "He's your true mate, Ember. You only get one, and you always hear there's an option to break it, but I don't know anyone who's found their mate and actually been able to go through with breaking the bond. I wouldn't even know how you go about that."

"But it's not like I'm in love with him or anything. I mean, I like him well enough. He was surprisingly easy to talk to, but love? Don't you need love to make a lifetime commitment?"

"I don't know. My grandmother says friendship is the number one most important thing, and that with friendship comes love. Not the fleeting, all-consuming kind, but the sort of love that lasts a lifetime through not just the good times, but the bad ones."

"There's something to be said for that, I guess."

The door to my room opened and Magenta walked in. I quickly shot Melissa a look of panic. She smiled and made a silent motion of sealing her lips. I laughed and hugged her. I was really grateful she took the time to try to get to know me this semester. It was nice having someone to talk to.

Magenta rolled her eyes when she saw us, but she was alone for once. Without a word, she changed and climbed into bed.

Melissa said goodbye and let herself out and I went back to bed too.

I replayed her words over and over in her head.

I'm glad you found someone to talk to, Chad said softly through our bond.

Even being in the dark, mostly alone, I blushed furiously.

You aren't supposed to listen in on everything, I reminded him.

I wasn't trying to. You were just broadcasting it pretty loudly, he teased.

I was not, I insisted.

Were too, he retaliated.

I giggled and heard Magenta huff and turn over in her bed.

You're making me laugh and my roommate is getting pissed.

Oh please, like that's anything new. Bet it doesn't take much to piss her off.

I fought back a fit of giggles. Settling down, I confessed, *I'm glad Melissa was around to talk to tonight. She's a good friend.*

I'm glad too. You need more friends like her. Speaking of which, Karis and Jenna called tonight. They really want to meet you and probably aren't going to leave me alone until I introduce you. Would you be interested in heading over to the cabin Friday night?

I don't know, where is that?

Oh, Chase and Jenna own a cabin, actually a really big house in the woods a few miles off campus. I can arrange to get us there if you don't want to drive, though I promise that no one there will care what we arrive in, as long as we get there. They're moving at the end of the semester and Damon and Karis are taking over the house. They've already mostly moved in. Just my luck, he said.

What do you mean?

I transferred here last semester. Chase was my first roommate, but he was in the middle of mating and moved out when he bought the cabin for her. There was a lot of shit that went down between the dogs and the big cats.

I heard about that, I confessed.

Yeah, it was sort of the talk of campus for a while. One of our brothers died in a battle defending them. He was Damon's roommate, and afterwards he couldn't stand to stay in that room.

So he moved in with you, but found his true mate and moved out too? I guessed.

Yeah, that's the gist of it. But hey, if you ever need a hideout from Magenta, I know a place. It's not exactly the library, but there's a spare bed for you.

I felt like he was joking, but I couldn't really tell. *Didn't he say strictly platonic?* I thought without realizing I'd just broadcasted my thoughts to him through the bond. I knew my face was probably beet red. I waited to see if he'd respond.

You're welcome over here anytime, he finally said. *Sweet dreams, Ember.*

Goodnight.

Chad

Chapter 9

Getting to know Ember may have been a mistake. She wasn't just cute, she was fun and easy to talk to. She didn't like pretenses and that had been a big pet peeve of mine throughout the spring and summer out here. It was like California was on a whole new level compared to the East Coast. I didn't know how else to explain it.

The fact that she wasn't a squirrel still bothered me, but less than I thought it should. Heck, I still didn't even know what she was. Mom was going to freak when she found out, but as the week went by and we talked more and more I wasn't sure how long I'd handle this platonic thing we had going on. I was ready to claim her as mine. Sometimes the feeling was almost more than I could handle. I had a mate; just that thought kept a smile on my face.

It had taken some convincing, but I finally got her to agree to go to the cabin with me. I tried to assure her it wasn't going to be some wild party, but in truth I never knew what to expect when the beer came out around my brothers. Chase and Damon both had invited us to stay the night Friday. I didn't even know how to mention it to Ember.

You could try just asking, she said sarcastically. *You know when you stress out you start sharing your thoughts. I'm trying to take a test here.*

Do you want to stay the night over there then? I asked.

58

If I say yes will you go away and let me finish this test in peace?

I'll try, I said.

Fine then, we'll stay. Now go away.

I was sitting in the common room at the house and couldn't stop grinning.

"Cut it out already. You look like a cat who swallowed a canary," Brett said. "It's bad enough I have to put up with Chase and Damon, but now you too?"

I shrugged.

"So, things are going well with Ember then?" he pressed.

"We'll see. We're taking it slow and just getting to know each other."

"But you like her," Brett said.

I grinned. "Yeah, I do," I admitted.

"She coming to the cabin with you this weekend?"

"Yup. Took some convincing, but I finally wore her down."

"Finally, someone who doesn't fall at your feet and beg to have your babies. I like her already," Brett joked.

I shoved him off the arm of the couch where he was sitting. He landed on the floor with a thump, drawing the attention of some of the other brothers.

"Hey, what's up?" Jackson asked.

"Nothing," I said a little too quickly.

"Just messing around with Chad," Brett said, clearly taking my queue not to blab about my personal business. Not that anything stayed secret for long in the doghouse. For now, I just wanted to keep Ember to myself. I knew come Friday night that would all be gone as I would have to introduce her around.

Knowing how much she hated the spotlight, I was a little nervous about it. She had to know what she was walking into though. I wasn't bragging by saying I was one of the most popular guys on campus. That would usually tame down some over the coming months; it always did in the winter, but these girls were a whole different breed than I was used to, so I couldn't be certain of that.

I saw Ember on Wednesday, but she had a paper to write Thursday night and asked me not to bother her. I'd obeyed, but that meant I didn't get to see her again until Friday night. I had planned to pick her up at her dorm and walk over to her car. She'd agreed to drive, and I was glad as it gave us a few minutes together.

At the last minute she told me Magenta had friends in the room and she'd just meet me at the house. It felt a little like she was picking me up for a date, though I had promised her it wasn't a date. But let's be real, I was taking my mate to meet my fraternity brothers. This was a little more important to me than just a date. I just didn't want to let on how much though.

I was waiting on the porch for Ember to arrive. She had told me through the bond that she was on her way. Several girls had passed by and tried to talk to me, but I'd simply dismissed them as politely as I could. I saw another approaching from the corner of my eye and turned away. Ember should be there any second and I didn't want the distraction.

"Well, are we going or what?" the girl asked, and I turned slowly recognizing her voice immediately.

She was wearing tight designer jeans with a few holes, boots with a heel, and a crop top that not only showed off defined abs but was cut low enough to make my eyes water. Her hair was swept up, exposing the long slender column of her neck, and she wasn't wearing glasses. Her makeup was done to perfection. I stared at the vision before me in shock.

"What?" she finally asked.

"Uh, you just look so different," I said sounding like a bumbling idiot.

She rolled her eyes. "You said it was a party. I do know how to be presentable when I need to."

I grinned. Same smartass mouth I was growing to love. *Like, not love*, I reminded myself.

"You're going to show me up tonight," I said.

"What? You can't handle all the attention not being on you?" she teased.

"I hate the attention, and so do you," I reminded her. It was definitely something we had in common.

"But you know when it's necessary and when it's not. I prefer looser jeans and a T-shirt, but well, you do know who my mother is. She did drill some sense of fashion into me," she said.

"I'm glad," I said. "Though I do miss the flannel. It was starting to grow on me."

She laughed and shoved me away as we walked to her car.

"Seriously though, you look beautiful tonight," I said. I could feel how happy that made her, and I tried not to let it freak me out. It was too soon. I shouldn't be feeling her emotions this early.

"Thanks," she said in a breathy voice.

I grabbed her bag as she opened the garage and popped the trunk. She stood and watched as I put both our bags in and shut it.

"Um, would you like to drive this time? I don't have a clue where we're going."

"Are you sure?" I asked. It was a really nice car and I didn't want to mess it up.

"I wouldn't offer if I wasn't," she said. I loved that she had such a smart mouth, always ready with a witty comeback.

I took the keys, but first walked to the passenger side and opened the door for her. She smiled at me but refrained from commenting. I knew how to be a gentleman when I needed to.

I jogged around to the driver's side and climbed in. First, I adjusted the seat and mirrors, then fired it up. Man was it a nice car.

Ember was quiet on the drive over.

"Are you okay?" I asked as I turned on to the driveway to the cabin.

"I'm fine," she said, but I wasn't buying it. "Okay, it's my first college party. I'm a little nervous."

I reached over and linked my fingers between hers. I wasn't prepared for the jolt of awareness that shot through me from the simple touch. "This is sort of like a family event more than a typical party, and I'll be right here the entire time."

She turned serious eyes to me. "Is that supposed to make me feel better?"

I laughed as I let go of her hand and got out of the car. I made it to her side before she could open her door. I held out my hand and she took it. This time I was ready for the physical punch it caused.

"I was kind of hoping it would ease your mind a little bit at least," I joked.

She shook her head at me and remained quiet as we walked up to the house. The first thing I noticed was that she didn't gawk or comment on the size of the cabin. Everyone I knew who had been there had stopped in front in shock, but not Ember. It was the first moment it really hit me that she was Alicia Kenston's daughter and way out of my league. This cabin looked enormous to me and was probably the size of her pool house. Did she have a pool house?

Ember laughed and leaned over to whisper. "Yes, we have a pool house."

"Shit!"

The front door flew open and Damon walked out. "Hey, Chad and Ember are here," he announced.

"Chad!" the room roared.

"Whoa, who is that?" Jackson asked as we entered.

"Back off, she's taken," Brett warned him.

"Who is she?" he asked. "I don't think I've ever seen her around campus before. Trust me, I'd remember her."

I stiffened, ready to challenge him right then and there. If I were a wolf, I'd be growling at him. But there were limitations being a squirrel shifter, and sometimes I just couldn't pull off that same level of intimidation.

"Karis is dying to meet you. Let me go grab her," Damon said. "Just ignore those guys. They won't bother you here," he added, loud enough to get the point across for me.

"Whoa, yeah, of course not. Hi, I'm Jackson," he said, extending his hand out to Ember.

I had to let go of her hand so that she could shake his. I was surprised by how agitated that brief gesture made my squirrel.

"Ember. It's nice to meet you," she said politely. As soon as he let go, she linked her fingers with mine once again.

I chanced a quick look at her, and she smiled up at me. It was like she knew I needed her touch.

When Damon came back he had not only Karis, but Chase and Jenna too.

"Hi Ember, I'm Jenna, this is my mate Chase," she said first.

"And this is my mate, Karis," Damon said proudly.

"Hi, it's nice to meet you all," Ember returned.

Chase was giving me a curious look. At first chance he pulled me aside. "Dude, are you okay?"

"No, I'm not okay," I said through gritted teeth. "Why didn't you assholes tell me how hard it would be to have her around unmated males?"

Chase burst out laughing. "Sorry, I thought that was a given."

"What's so funny?" Damon asked.

"Our boy is having some territorial issues," Chase said.

"Oh, that. Yeah, it sucks. Parties are the worst," Damon said. "It gets better after you seal the bond, so I wouldn't recommend taking too long on that."

"We're keeping things platonic and getting to know each other," I told them in a low voice.

"You were holding hands when you came in. I figured things were escalating," Damon admitted.

I shook my head. "She's not a squirrel," I told them.

"Well shit, you're really going to let that come between you?" Chase asked. "What is she then?"

I shrugged. "I don't know, but not a squirrel."

"You're an idiot if you let that come between you," Chase said before walking away.

"Don't look at me. I agree with him," Damon said.

I looked around and saw Ember surrounded by Jenna and Karis. They were laughing about something and just looked and felt so right having her there. Was I really an idiot to let something like that come between us?

Jackson walked over and clapped his hand on my shoulder. "You could have warned us," he said.

"About what?"

"Your mate. I've been around long enough to know that look."

"What look?" I asked wondering just how much he'd had to drink already.

"The mated look. The nothing else in this world suddenly matters but that girl you can't keep your eyes off of look. Someday, maybe I'll be lucky enough to have it, but I've had enough friends fall to the bonding call to recognize that look. Plus, you sort of put off a stench. Did you know that?" he asked.

"What?" I asked trying to discreetly smell my pits. I'd taken a shower before we got there. I didn't stink.

"I'm serious. Some sort of weird pheromone. It stands out more because I've never smelled it before, but when you were getting territorial back there, Brett and I both noticed it."

"Shit. Do you think Ember noticed?" I asked.

Damon shrugged. "Chances are she'd like the smell if she did. Usually with scents it's designed to call to your mate while warning off competition."

"Awe, you thought I was competition?" Jackson teased.

"Shut up," I warned, and saw Damon crinkle his nose.

"Yup, Jackson's right. You're scenting," Damon said.

"Shit. How do I stop it?" I asked.

"Probably can't, man. Don't worry about it. We'll discreetly spread the word and warn the others. Karis and Jenna will take care of Ember when you're not around," Damon said.

"Okay," I agreed, feeling grateful that these guys always had my back.

I walked back over to Ember. She turned and smiled as I approach, and it did something inside of me. I felt exhilarated just from one look.

"Hey, can I get you a drink or something?" I asked her.

"We have pretty much anything you could possibly want," Jenna added.

"Um, sure. A beer, I guess," she said. I raised a curious eyebrow to her. "Fine a Coke, if we're not drinking. I don't care."

She had told me she didn't drink much, so I had been surprised she'd request a beer. I headed for the kitchen and quickly returned with a cup of beer and a can of Coke. I offered both to her.

She laughed and took them both. "Well, I won't need another drink for a while."

Ember seemed to be getting along great with the girls, so I left her to mingle around the room. I liked knowing the girls were watching out for her. I'd seen both Damon and Chase pull their mates away long enough to ask them to stay with my mate.

My mate? When did I start becoming so territorial over Ember? *Shit, I swore this wouldn't happen.*

What's wrong? she asked, sounding genuinely concerned.

Nothing, I said, trying make it sound believable. In truth, everything was wrong. I wasn't just being territorial over her, I was falling for her. Fast and hard.

Ember

Chapter 10

I was surprised by just how much I liked Jenna and Karis.
They both seemed like genuinely nice people. There were no airs
about them. They welcomed me with open arms and told me several
times how happy they were that Chad had found me. I didn't have
the heart to tell them we were only friends.

Most of the party was outside in the backyard, but people
came and went coming back inside for drinks and snacks. We stayed
inside. Chad had gone off with some of his friends. I'd only been
introduced to a few people which seemed weird. It also felt like the
girls were keeping me from really joining in which seemed even
weirder, but I honestly didn't mind it.

We eventually wound our way through the house as Jenna
led me on a tour, then settled down on the couches in the living
room.

"Okay, I'm dying to know. What's it like having Chad in
your head all the time? I mean that really is a thing, right? He said
squirrel shifters pick up telepathy with their mates first. Is that true?
I'm a wolf, that's like final stages for me," Karis said.

I laughed. "Yup, apparently that's true. Honestly it
completely freaked me out at first, but you grow used to it. When we
get stressed, upset, or let our guard down we start to broadcast

information we didn't mean to share. Both of us have done it. It's going to take some practice to fix that, but it hasn't been too much trouble so far."

"We are so happy Chad found you. He's such a great guy, fearless. You should see him in battle," Jenna said with a laugh.

"I'm just glad he found another squirrel shifter," Karis said, rolling her eyes.

"Oh, I'm not a squirrel," I said. They shared a worried look. "It's okay," I told them. "I know how he feels about that. For some reason he wanted to get to know me anyway. We're honestly just friends, we aren't encouraging the bond. He plans on breaking it, whatever that means. I still don't understand it all."

"No he won't," Jenna said with certainty. "So if you're banking on him breaking your bond, you better prepare for disappointment, and if you want it broken, then you better walk away quickly."

I was taken back by the sudden change in her voice. I tried not to take it personally. She was clearly very protective of Chad. "He's made it pretty clear he's going to break it," I told her.

She gave a short laugh. "He also walked in and scented the whole damn house to warn off any other male in the area from coming near you."

"What?" I sniffed the air, but only smelled a pleasant woodsy scent that warmed my body all over. I liked it. I thought it was some sort of natural smelling candle or something.

Karis laughed at my surprise. "You smell something pleasant in the air, don't you?"

"Well, yeah, I smelled it when we first walked in. It's nice," I admitted.

Karis smiled at me. "It's supposed to be nice. . .for you. Just for you. It's pretty cold out tonight, but there's a reason most everyone is staying outdoors."

The two of them laughed harder.

"Sorry," Jenna said. "It's not the most pleasant smell for the rest of us. Not nearly as strong to our senses, but to the males, yeah, it downright stinks. If there was any doubt in anyone's mind that Chad was claiming you as his, it was put to rest when the two of you walked in."

I wondered what had changed between us. Why hadn't he said anything? And what did it mean for me? For us? So many questions going through my mind. He said we were just going to be friends. Had that changed now too? I was trying not to freak out. It had been so much to take in. Even though I'd been able to compartmentalize everything, this was blurring those lines I'd formed, and I didn't know what to do about it.

"Hey, are you okay?" Karis asked. "I know that look of panic. You haven't had anyone to talk about this stuff with, have you?"

"Talk about it? No. I mean my friend Melissa, but she's never gone through it and thinks it's the most romantic thing in the world. I tried to tell her that's not the case, but she thinks I'm crazy. I didn't even know there was such a thing till it happened to me."

"What? Are you serious?" Karis asked.

I nodded sadly.

"Come on, let's go. I'm officially changing this to ladies' night. Follow me," Jenna said getting up and walking to the back of the house. "Anyone need a drink?"

"I'm good," I said.

"Me too," Karis said lifting her glass. "Don't worry, Ember. Everything's going to be just fine. Jenna really helped me through it not that long ago. If you have any questions, feel free to ask. No judgement here. You can say or question anything you'd like."

"Hold on," Jenna said walking around the large bed in the room they'd led me to. She flipped a switch on some strange looking device sitting on the nightstand. "Okay, we're good. You're free to talk openly now."

"What's that?" I asked.

"A dampener," she said. "It's designed to give privacy. Wolves especially have super hearing, even in their skin. This puts a shield of protection around us so they can't hear through it. Anything we say in here is completely confidential."

I liked the sound of that. I hadn't had any true friends to confide in for a long time. Okay, maybe never. Those I'd thought were my friends had turned on me over a boy in high school. Ever since I'd been leery of talking to other girls about anything. I'd made an exception for only a few and most recently, Melissa.

"Okay, so you really hadn't heard about the mating process? Like at all?" Karis asked.

I shook my head.

"But how is that even possible? Someone should have prepared you for this," she said, sounding upset and I realized she was upset for me.

"I'm, well, I'm adopted." I sighed. I was going to have to tell them. "My parents are humans. Only a few people know that, so please don't go spreading it around."

"Humans? You were raised by humans?"

I nodded. "Trust me they were just as surprised as I was the first time I shifted, but I guess I'm lucky. They love me unconditionally. I don't know how I'd have survived without them."

"How'd you even find this place?" Karis asked curiously. "I mean it's not like you can just google shifter colleges and Archibald Reynolds appears. Very few people even know about this place."

"Um, my dad. He, uh, he sort of knows things. He helped me a lot, but he never mentioned anything about this mating stuff. Why didn't he tell me?"

"He probably doesn't know about it or doesn't understand it." Jenna said.

She pulled out her phone and scrolled through pictures, then handed it to me. "Does he wear a ring like this?"

I looked at the picture and my eyes went wide. I slowly nodded.

"Verndari. Did he know all along what you are?"

"No. He was just as shocked as I was when it happened, but at least he knew what was going on with me. You aren't going to say anything, are you? I know humans aren't supposed to know about us." That was my biggest fear in mentioning my parents were human, that someone like Karis would be smart enough to put it all together and ask questions.

"The Verndari are sort of an exception to that rule," Jenna assured me. "I know a few of them. Most of them are pretty cool."

"My dad's the best," I said proudly.

"I'm glad you had him, but he probably doesn't understand the whole true mates thing. Even if he did, different species get the signs in different orders, so for me," Karis said, "wolves are about as opposite of squirrels as possible. Telepathy is basically the last sign before a sealed bond and takes years, often decades to achieve."

"And since he's a squirrel and you're not, that can screw things up even further. Chase and I found that out first hand because his wolf signs were slightly differed from my panther signs and we ended up with both simultaneously. No one had prepared us for that either," Jenna confessed.

"What is your spirit animal anyway?" Karis finally asked.

I sighed. "A chipmunk." They had such awesome animal spirits and mine was just a cute little chipmunk.

They both looked at each other and then burst out laughing. "Aren't they in the same family as squirrels?"

I shrugged. "I don't know. Similar I guess."

"Does Chad know what you are?"

I thought about it for a second and then shook my head. "Probably not. He only ever asked if I was a squirrel."

They laughed even harder.

"And you said no?" Jenna asked.

"Of course, I'm not a squirrel, I'm a chipmunk."

"Poor guy. You're likely tormenting him for nothing. That's basically the same thing," Karis said.

Jenna sobered. "You never know. I mean black panthers and jaguars are basically the same animal just different coats, but that certainly would not be acceptable by my father's standards."

I heard the disdain in her voice. I'd heard enough around campus about her and Chase to understand why that bothered her so much.

"Anyway, just like Chase and Jenna couldn't stay away from each other despite her father, I highly doubt that Chad's going to be able to cave to his mother's wishes now that he's found you. The mating call is designed to lure you in and push the two of you together," Karis explained.

"So I have no choice in this?" I asked.

"It's not really like that, but then again it doesn't feel good when you try to walk away either."

"Yeah, the rejection causes physical pain. It's awful. Plus, there's a reason you were paired with Chad, Ember. Once you get to know him and you find those little things that are unique to just the two of you, it's really hard to walk away from that," Jenna added.

"Why would you want to? I mean, we're talking about one man perfectly designed just for you. Trust me, I get it. I had a lot riding on my shoulders. I couldn't risk just anyone as my mate, and at first glance Damon was never going to cut it. I was wrong. I kept us at arms' length for longer than was necessary because I was scared, but if I'd just put my trust in our bond, things would have gone a lot easier," Karis said.

"Karis is an heir, which means whoever she mated would someday rule her Pack as Alpha. It's sort of a really big deal, so she needed to be cautious," Jenna explained.

"I haven't fought this? My head's been swimming and I feel like I'm just treading water here at times, but I've been going with it. I don't even understand what's happening really," I confessed.

"That's good," Jenna assured me. "Just see what happens. I mean Chad's a great guy, like really awesome. We all love him. He came in and just fit right in. He has his little quirks, but who doesn't?"

Karis laughed. "His chip fetish drives Damon nuts!"

"Chip fetish?" I asked.

"Yeah, apparently he loves chips and hides bags of them everywhere in his room. Damon would move them around just to drive him nuts. He's seriously territorial over those chips."

"Yes, do not mess with that boy's chips!" Jenna laughed. "Chase used to comment on it too."

"You know that's normal for our kind, right?" I asked, trying to see what the big deal was. "I tend to compartmentalize things, not necessarily as specific as chips, but, well, everything. My roommate is a bit of a pig, especially if she's not expecting company and it drives me crazy. Everything should have a spot, or you just don't need it."

They looked at me and grinned.

"See this is what I was trying to say," Karis said. "Those little quirks that may drive others crazy are perfect for you, because he's perfect for you."

"But he said he didn't want me, not in the way you guys are talking," I said as I finished the last of my beer and wished I had another. I opened the can of Coke instead.

The girls gave each other another shared look. I was envious of their closeness.

"He lied," they said in unison and then cracked up laughing.

"He probably didn't know he was lying, but trust us, he wants you as far more than just a friend," Jenna added.

That one thought stayed with me for the remainder of the night. We'd finished up our talk and decided to join the party. Chad visibly relaxed when he saw me. I gave him a short wave. Could they be right? Were things changing between us?

I couldn't tell for sure, but I was so intrigued by the concept and how romantic and perfect Melissa had made it seem that a strong part of me wanted to go for it and see what would happen. Or maybe that was the beer talking. I rarely drank alcohol and was definitely what people would call a light-weight. I already had a slight buzz just off the one drink, but I'd left my Coke in the bedroom and the second someone noticed I was empty-handed, another beer had been thrust upon me.

I was aware that Chad was keeping a close eye on me as he made his rounds throughout the room. He got uneasy anytime another male approached me. It was like I could feel it without even seeing him. Was that normal? Was that another stage of this mating stuff? I needed to remember to ask the girls when I got a chance.

I liked that he was a little jealous. It showed me he really did care, and maybe as more than just a friend. I had read so many books about soulmates and finding that one special person that of course my heart wanted to reach out and accept that. It was the foundation of every great fairytale and I was living it. But I was also grounded enough to know the difference between reality and make-believe, and this seemed to fall somewhere in the middle and was hard to grasp.

I vowed to just relax and have fun for the evening and see where things led. I liked Chad, a lot. I didn't think I would when I first met him. He was so popular and so handsome. I had noticed he'd put on a bit of weight. If I didn't monitor every bite this time of year, that happened to me too. Maybe it was a squirrel and chipmunk thing. Maybe our animals were a lot more alike than I'd first thought.

Somewhere outside music was playing, and I was drawn to it. I had always loved music, almost as much as I loved books. I emptied the rest of my glass, feeling a little freer as the alcohol set in, though I was still cognizant of all my actions.

Chad came over to check on me. It was the first time I'd been close enough to even talk to him since we'd arrived.

"Want to dance?" he asked.

"Yes," I said happily.

He took my hand and it felt like lightning shooting up my arm and straight to my gut. My whole body warmed from his touch. Drinking had always made me horny, but nothing like this. It was the first time I looked at Chad and saw more than just a friend, and I wanted him.

As we took the dance floor, pumping with energy, everything changed.

"Let's slow things down a bit on this beautiful night," the DJ said as a slow song filled the air.

Chad pulled me into his arms as we swayed to the music. I couldn't look him in the eyes because I knew he'd know instantly that I was starting to feel things for him that we said we weren't going to feel, and I was certain it wasn't just the alcohol talking.

You look beautiful tonight, he told me, choosing to speak through the bond.

So you've said, I teased.

I'm sorry I haven't been around much, but you disappeared with Jenna and Karis. I hope that went well, he said sounding a little uncomfortable.

They're great. We had a really good talk. They filled me in on some of the things that, well, you shouldn't have to about all this mating stuff, I confessed. I had consumed just enough to make my tongue looser than it should be. I knew my filter was off and hoped he didn't ask too many personal questions tonight.

Should I be concerned? His laughter filled my head.

I loved hearing him inside of me. It was a sudden realization that I had and broadcasted right back to him. It was comforting and made me feel safe.

He pulled back and grinned at me. "How much have you had to drink?"

I rolled my eyes at him. "Only two beers and that Coke. I'm done for the night. I know I'm a lightweight and I know better than to go over two. That's my limit."

He smiled, "Well, I'm glad you know your limit, but you're also letting your guard down and sending me all of your thoughts."

I blushed furiously. "So what? It's not like you don't already know you're hot," I blurted out. "Every other girl on campus has already told you as much. I'm sure your ego must be enormous," I said, but I didn't really believe it for a second, and worse, he knew I didn't believe it.

Maybe, he said through the bond, *but it's a lot nicer hearing it come from you.*

He pulled me closer and rubbed his hand up and down my back as we continued to dance. One slow song ended, and another was played. My body was pulsating uncomfortably. I needed him, I wanted him. I heard Chad gulp and knew I'd just told him as much. We had a room waiting just upstairs. We could sneak away, and no one would ever know. Desire filled me, and I knew only he could provide the relief I desperately wanted.

I felt his panic before I pulled back to see his face.

"What's wrong?" I asked.

He shook his head. *Not here.*

I could feel how much he physically wanted me too. There was no doubt in my mind it was a mutual desire. With him pressed so closely against me, it took little for my imagination to take over.

He let his guard down as his emotions heightened. His desire combined with mine and it was amazing and unreal, and then he let go of probably his biggest secret. I froze. Chad was still a virgin. I pulled back and stared at him in shock.

"How is that even possible?"

I saw the color drain from his cheeks as he looked around. I took a deep breath and wrapped my arms around him. My head was swimming with that knowledge. I loved knowing that I was going to be his first, and there was not a single doubt in my mind that it was going to happen. And then the guilt hit me. Why hadn't I waited for him too?

It was late in the night and many of his brothers had already headed home. I suspected most of those left were likely staying the night. I was also suddenly aware that Chase and Jenna as well as Karis and Damon were dancing nearby but watching us.

Jenna left and returned with the funny little device she'd called the dampener. She handed it to me and hugged me. "Looks like you two need to talk, or something. This will give you privacy. Chad already took your bags up to your room."

I nodded, "Thanks, Jenna."

I turned and headed for the stairs holding onto Chad's hand. No way was he getting away from me tonight.

Chad

Chapter 11

Ember was leading me up to the bedroom. Damon and Chase had said there were a lot of people staying over and they needed the other spare rooms. I thought that was just because they were trying to push us together, and I had left my stuff in the room to get them off my back but had planned to just sleep on the couch downstairs. Now everything was moving faster than I could keep up.

At the top of the stairs she hesitated, but I knew it was only because she didn't know which room ours was. I took the lead and showed her the way, opening the door so she could enter first. In my world it was a sign of respect. In the wolf world I knew it was the ultimate sign of respect and submission. I hesitated, trying to discern which I was portraying. I shook my head to clear it and followed her in, shutting the door behind me.

"Do you know how this thing works?" she asked.

"Yeah, here, I'll take care of it," I told her.

I took the dampener from her and plugged it into the wall, then turned it on. Unease filled me. I didn't know what to say to her. We were alone in a bedroom, and my body definitely knew what it wanted, which only added to my nerves.

Ember sat on the bed as I stood awkwardly staring at her. When she rose, still silently watching me almost like she was seeing me for the first time, I quickly closed the gap between us. I wasn't thinking, only feeling, when I reached out and pulled her close to me. My lips sought hers in a searing kiss that shot heat straight to my groin.

I could feel her emotions as real as my own, and it caused feelings within me that I couldn't even put into words. It was incredible, amazing, and for the first time in my life I didn't want it to end. I had waited my entire life for this moment.

"Do we need to talk about it?" Ember asked as she broke away to fumble with the buttons on my shirt.

"Does it bother you?" I asked, understanding she was talking about my virginity.

"Not at all. Why should it?" she asked.

I shrugged, then smiled and leaned in to kiss her again.

"This is going to change things," I warned her.

"According to Jenna and Karis things are already changing. I can feel you, not just hear you in my head. They said that was a sign our bond was already growing. Can you feel me too?"

I nodded. "Yeah, I can, but I need this to be your decision. A bond, Ember, that's everything. It means a lifetime together. We just met. I don't want to rush you," I told her honestly.

Her hands stilled on the last button. She looked deep into my eyes. "Right this second all I know is that I desperately need you. Only you," she said.

That was it. Pleasing my parents, giving her more time, trying to do the right thing, none of it mattered. I pushed all thoughts away and was left with only desire.

Her pupils dilated as she recognized my change. I kissed her again as my tongue swept past her lips and swirled with hers. She moaned against my mouth and I smiled. Lost in kissing her, my hands seemed to have a mind of their own. I gently caressed the soft skin beneath her shirt. When I reached the hem, I lifted it up, breaking our kiss only long enough to remove it before continuing my explorations.

She shoved my shirt off of my shoulders and down my arms, then quickly discarded the T-shirt beneath it. She took a step back and carefully looked me over. I had never felt so exposed and desperately wanted to know what she was thinking.

Open your mind to me, I prompted.

Her eyes widened, but then she nodded. *Better?*

"Much."

God, he's way hotter than I imagined.

Her praise empowered me. I reached around and unclipped her bra, letting it fall to the floor at our feet. She wasn't bashful in the least, and that was something that surprised me a little.

I left her lips to trail kisses across her cheek and down the slender column of her neck as her breasts filled the palms of my hands. *Perfect.*

She moaned as I toyed with her. *That feels so good.*

I continued kissing my way down her body as I picked her up and then gently laid her down on the bed. I may not have had sex yet, but I'd been this far. I knew how to please her, and if there were any doubts, her praise and guidance through our open bond made it easy to know just what she needed.

I stopped at her navel to swirl my tongue around her belly button as my fingers fumbled with the button of her jeans.

Lift up for me, I told her, and she obeyed so I could slide them down her legs. I stood up and stared down at her, taking my time to appreciate my mate for the first time. *So beautiful.*

The blush that started in her cheeks spread to her chest. I had never seen anything so gorgeous as my mate needy and wanting for me.

Please, Chad, she begged.

Shit, I didn't come prepared for this, I thought, not meaning to let it slip through our bond.

It's okay, you're obviously clean, so am I. Plus I'm on the pill. We're good.

I gulped. This was really happening. *At least I don't have to fumble with a condom while my hands are shaking.*

She giggled. This time it was my turn to blush. I covered up my embarrassment by getting back to her needs. Focusing on that helped calm my nerves. I carefully slid the cotton underwear she wore down her legs fully exposing her to me. My heart raced. This was already further than I'd ever gone before, but I at least had some idea of what needed to be done.

I grinned up at her as I leaned over and kissed her in her most private place. She propped up on her elbows to stare down at me, so I began to tease her until her hips bucked against me.

Yes!

That simple word was all the encouragement I needed. I began aggressively exploring her more intimately. I quickly learned the places she liked and was surprised to find that I was getting harder off of her desire. When I hit the right spot, she cried out my name.

"Chad!" I heard it both aloud and in my head. It was like the ultimate rush. *Don't stop. Right there,* she directed me.

I looked up just in time to see her head drop back as her thighs tightened around me. I didn't hesitate or give her time to come down from her orgasm before I sat up, quickly discarded the remainder of my own clothes and positioned myself between her legs.

Our eyes locked and I gulped as I eased inside her. It was the most natural feeling in the entire world being there like that with Ember. I froze, staring down at her, overwhelmed by the emotions.

Just breathe. And move slowly at first. We'll find our groove, she patiently guided me.

As I followed her command and slowly pulled out, then back in again with her praise and directions, I quickly grew confident. Having her inside my head like that and the sensations we were creating quickly became intense both physically and emotionally. We were in perfect harmony and it was the greatest feeling in the world.

Mine, I growled as I picked up the pace.

The more she cried my name, the headier I became. It was intoxicating.

I'm so close, she warned me.

I wasn't sure if she said anything further, or I just felt her needs, but leaned down and sucked one of her nipples into my mouth and she broke our rhythm with sporadic jerks. As she came, hard, her orgasm clenched around me and I was powerless to stop the effect as I followed her over the edge.

Sweaty and gasping for breath, I leaned down and kissed her softly.

"Holy shit that was amazing!" she said making me feel like a god in the bedroom.

I rolled off her, worried my weight was too much. My limbs felt weak and my chest heaved as I tried to catch my breath and regain control of my emotions. They were so mixed up with Ember's I wasn't sure which of us was feeling what.

"No one warned me it would be like that," I admitted.

She laughed. "That's because that was not normal. No way was that your first time."

I beamed with pride. Having the bond open fully between us had made things easy for me. I had no doubt it also was a far more intimate experience than I ever would have had with anyone else.

I'm glad I waited. You were worth it.

I did not bother to get dressed, but then pulled back the sheets and settled into bed. Ember followed my lead and I tugged her closer to cuddle her through the night. I could feel the bond between us growing stronger.

Ember

Chapter 12

Waking up in Chad's arms felt so right that it scared the shit out of me. I had driven him over, or I probably would have snuck out and bailed. I needed some alone time to process what had happened.

I'd had a couple beers, but I hadn't been drunk. I wanted that. I wanted him, but I had been tipsy enough to not consider the consequences of my actions.

Chad stiffened next to me.

"Are you okay?" he asked without even opening his eyes. "It sort of feels like you're freaking out."

"Maybe a little," I admitted.

He frowned and opened his eyes to stare into mine. "You're having second thoughts?"

Now he was starting to freak out. I could feel his emotions as clearly as if they were my own. I didn't want to upset him. I just needed some time to let it all sink in. Everything was changing so quickly. I didn't handle change well.

I either told him as much without meaning to or he felt my needs, either way I couldn't take the sadness in his eyes.

"I need to get back. I have some work to do before I head home this week," I said. It wasn't a lie, but it also wouldn't take me long to do it. Studying and focusing on anything but the man whose arms were wrapped around me would help distract me from how he made me feel safe and wanted, desired even. I wasn't used to these emotions. I wasn't used to people noticing me, and I felt too vulnerable lying there naked beside him knowing he truly saw me, the real me, because I could never hide anything from him.

"Okay," he said climbing out of bed and reaching for his pants. "I'll give you a few minutes to get dressed. I'll be downstairs when you're ready."

He left and the sadness he felt made me miserable.

I grabbed my bag and a fresh change of clothes. After dressing I headed for the attached bathroom. I looked a wreck. This was why I didn't drink. I scrubbed my face clean, removed the contacts I was wearing and put my glasses back on. I brushed through my hair, then pulled out a beanie to cover it. The jeans, the flannel shirt, the hat, the glasses, it all made me feel like me again.

Last night I'd felt like someone else entirely, even though I knew, I knew that I had never been more open and honestly me with anyone, than I'd been with Chad. I think that scared me more than anything else.

I grabbed my bag, noticing his was still there, and headed downstairs. Chad was talking with Chase and I knew he was upset. He couldn't hide his emotions from me. Like it or not, we were linked now. Intellectually I understood it. Emotionally, nothing made sense anymore. I couldn't just put him or what I was feeling for him into my neat little compartments.

"You ready?" he asked when he saw me standing at the bottom of the stairs.

I nodded without a word. Jenna walked out of her room still looking groggy. She frowned. "You're leaving already?

"Yeah, I've got work to do," I explained.

She walked over and hugged me. "I hate professors who load up last minute work for Thanksgiving week. We should have the entire week off." I smiled and nodded my agreement. "If I don't see you before you leave, have a great holiday and we'll catch up for coffee, or rather tea," she added remembering I'd told her I didn't drink coffee but was addicted to hot tea.

Speaking of which, Chad handed me a hot cup of tea in a travel mug. I took a long sip and started to relax. It was perfect. He was perfect. So why was I running away?

Chad said goodbye for the both of us and we turned to leave. Outside I noticed he still didn't have his stuff.

"Don't you want to grab your things?" I asked.

He shrugged. "I'll get it later. You seem like you're in a hurry to get back."

Ouch. That little comment stung, mainly because of the truth of it.

He drove us back and the silence between us was agonizing. I wanted to talk to him, but I was still sorting it all out myself and didn't know how to explain that without hurting him further. Still, he was the perfect gentlemen. He parked at the Dean's house and ran around to grab my door for me. He insisted on walking me back to my dorm, saying he knew I was upset, and that he'd feel better if he knew I had made it back safe and sound, but the tension between us still hurt.

When we finally reached my dorm room, music was blaring out into the hall and I knew Magenta was entertaining once again. I turned to Chad and we just stared at each other. I started to speak, to apologize for my behavior, and try to explain, but the door flew open.

Magenta. Her face went from surprise to happiness. Completely ignoring me, she gushed over Chad.

"Chad! I'm so glad you came. I wasn't sure you would."

My eyes went wide with hurt as I turned to look at him.

"I don't know what you're talking about," he said.

"Didn't you get my text?" she asked.

"No," he insisted. "I was just walking Ember home." Completely ignoring her, he turned to me. His look penetrated my soul. "Call me later?"

He looked simultaneously possessive and unsure of himself. I nodded. Then he shocked the hell out of me and pulled me into his arms and kissed me.

I know you're scared and need some time, but I'm here if you want to talk.

I pulled back to look at him and nodded before he turned to leave. I could feel his hesitation to do so, but I was glad he did.

"You are unbelievable," Magenta said. I knew she would be pissed, but she looked hurt too. I didn't have time to care. I walked into my room, threw down my duffle bag and grabbed my backpack instead. Ignoring everyone else in the room, I left without a word.

"Where do you think you're running off to?" Magenta said as I hit the hallway. She was still standing out there stunned.

"Don't worry, you have the room to yourself for a while," I told her.

"Uh-uh, you are not getting off that easy, you little bitch. You play all innocent around here, the poor misunderstood loner. How the hell did you land Chad?"

"That's really none of your business. Get out of my way," I said as she blocked my path.

"Not a chance until you tell me what the hell is going on around here."

At this point she was yelling and others on our floor started peeking their heads out of their rooms to see what all the commotion was about.

"That's enough. You're causing a scene," I told her.

"So what? Poor little Ember who pretends she doesn't want to be noticed is finally getting shown for what you really are? A whore, Ember. That's what you are."

I was done. My hands were on my hips and I squared off my shoulders. "Shut the hell up, Magenta. Everyone on this floor knows who the whore is, and it's certainly not me."

She was shooting daggers at me. I had never seen her so mad. "You'll pay for this, Ember. I'd watch my back if I were you," she said in a low tone that sent shivers through my body.

She stepped aside and walked back into our room.

I stared in shock for only a moment, then I ran straight to the library. I knew I was safe there, and Magenta had probably never even set foot in the place before, but my favorite place on campus, my sanctuary, did nothing but remind me of Chad. He was everywhere.

I needed to get out of there. By mid-afternoon my mind was made up. I had finished all my work for the short week, then emailed each of my professors, made all of the arrangements on how I would turn it in, and then I went back to my dorm room. Magenta was nowhere in sight and I was grateful I didn't have to face another show-down with her. I packed and left.

I needed to get the hell away from my crazy roommate, but more importantly, I needed a Chad free zone to figure things out.

When I arrived at home Mom and Dad were out. I felt bad that I was glad for it. I dragged my stuff up to my room and collapsed onto my bed. And then I cried. It was a good cleansing cry, the emotional outlet I needed. Unfortunately, I hadn't pulled myself together before my parents returned home.

"Ember?" Mom called, sounding worried. She opened my bedroom door and heard me sob. She ran to my bedside and wrapped me up in her arms. I had never doubted my parents love for even one second, but moments like this reminded me just how lucky I was to have them.

She didn't say a word, just held me. My dad peeked his head in and stood in the doorway watching us.

"Is she okay?" he finally asked my mother. I felt her shrug as she continued to cradle me.

I sobbed one last time and sat up, wiping my eyes. "I'm fine," I told them.

"Ember," my dad said in that tone that told me not to lie to him. I smiled. I'd missed them both so much, even though I'd been home just the weekend before, but it felt like a lifetime ago with everything that had happened.

"Daddy, why didn't you tell me about mating?" I asked.

His eyes grew wide and then he blushed. Despite everything, I laughed. My father who was larger than life and not afraid of anything was blushing because I mentioned mating. I guessed there was a reason Mom had been the one to give me the sex talk. You'd think as a scientist he could at least handle a clinical approach.

"Mating?" he asked uncomfortably. "Even after all these years of observation, we still don't have a full grasp on it. We know that the majority of shifters mate for life. And my friend Patrick told me they believe each shifter was paired with what they call their one true mate, handpicked by God. According to him there is nothing greater than finding your true mate. Is that what you're talking about? Or do you mean mating as in, um, uh, well, sex?"

In spite of it all, I laughed. "I know about sex, Dad. Mom and I had that talk when I was eleven. I lost my virginity in. . ."

"Ah, enough! Ember, I don't need that much information," he said holding his ears.

Mom laughed too. "To him you will always be his baby girl."

"Did you find your one true mate?" he asked.

I took in a deep breath and nodded.

"Is that why you're here and so upset?" Mom asked, and I nodded against her shoulder. "Ember, that's not something to be scared of. That should be exciting. You should be happy."

"Happy? I am, I guess. I'm not crying because I'm sad or upset. Chad's wonderful. I really like him, like a lot. It's just so much it's overwhelming me," I admitted. I already knew how they felt about my roommate, and I wasn't about to tell them about her threats. That contributed to my distress, but Chad was the more important of the two.

I felt a wave of fear come through the bond and I sat up, concerned.

What's wrong? I thought.

I stopped by the library to check on you, but you weren't there, so I went to your room. Did you really go home? Chad asked.

I sighed. *Yes. I'm at home. I just got overwhelmed. I'm talking to my parents about it now*, I confessed.

You're talking about us with them?

Of course. I can talk to them about anything. And I promise I'll talk to you later.

Are we okay, Ember? I could feel his sadness.

I smiled to myself. I hated that I was worrying him, but I liked knowing he cared that much. *Yeah, we're fine. I promise.*

I sniffed, already feeling better.

"Uh, what just happened?" Dad asked.

"You were crying and upset, then you just sat up and zoned out on us. Now you're smiling? Are you sure you're okay?" Mom asked, putting her hand to my forehead to make sure I wasn't sick with a fever.

I laughed and wiped my eyes. "I'm fine, or I'm going to be. Sorry, I left in a hurry. Chad was just worried and checking on me."

"Honey, you didn't even look at your phone," Mom pointed out.

"Oh, yeah, about that. Dad do you know about the signs of mating?" I asked, curious.

"What do you mean, sweetie?" he asked. I knew I had his full attention and I could tell by his curiosity that he had no idea what I was talking about.

"Did your friend Patrick tell you how you find your mate?"

He shook his head. "He mentioned something about how you just know."

I nodded. "Well apparently there are different stages to mating. Recognition is only one. There's this sort of bond that's created and it strengthens with time and causes crazy stuff to happen. It's really overwhelming. I know I've been saying that a lot, I just don't know how else to describe it. Apparently different species do things in different orders, but for my kind, we, um, we get a telepathic connection first. And I don't know if this is some shifter secret thing that I'm not supposed to be talking to you about, but I need to talk about it with someone," I said.

Dad was nearly bursting with questions and Mom kept assuring me that I could talk to them about absolutely anything. For the next two hours we sat there recapping it all as they helped me work through it. By the time we were done, I was emotionally spent. We had pizza delivered and I managed to eat a little before excusing myself and collapsing back into bed. It was the second most peaceful night of sleep I'd had, but still didn't compare to sleeping in Chad's arms.

The next morning I awoke feeling refreshed and ready to face my future. I knew Chad would be in class most of the day, so I went shopping with Mom and waited until I could call and really talk to him. He deserved that. I knew I was putting him through hell for nothing.

We were finishing up lunch when there was a knock at the front door.

"I'll get it," I yelled, feeling so much more like myself.

I swung the door open and my jaw dropped.

"Chad? What are you doing here?"

Chad

Chapter 13

I stood there looking at Ember. I hated how right I felt in her presence. I needed her, and I feared she was going to reject me. She had said we were okay, but she'd left, and I knew she'd been upset.

"I, uh, I was in the area and I just needed to see that you were okay," I told her honestly.

"I thought you had classes today."

"Just one this morning. I had already planned for my two that didn't cancel for tomorrow. Damon and Karis are flying home today. I just dropped them off at the airport. Damon loaned me his car for the week. I have to pick them up on Saturday" I explained. "You're not that far from the airport, so I thought I'd stop by to check on you before I head home."

I suddenly felt awkward. It had sounded like a good plan in my head, but now it came out needy and maybe a little stalkerish since she hadn't given me her home address. It was on the file Damon had pulled together on her. Maybe I was turning into an obsessed stalker.

I stared at the ground and scuffed the toe of my shoe across her welcome mat. I had almost changed my mind when I saw her neighborhood, and her house was the largest I'd seen. It was more than a little intimidating and reminded me of how very different we were. Ember was clearly out of my league.

She laughed, and I blushed realizing I'd just told her as much. She surprised me by wrapping her arms around my neck. "I'm glad you're here. I was going to call you this afternoon. I was just waiting until you got out of class."

"Really?" I asked.

I heard someone clear their throat behind her and she turned to look, then rolled her eyes. "Come on in. We'll talk, but first you have to meet my parents."

I gulped. *I hadn't considered that,* I admitted.

Ember laughed. "It's okay, they're dying to meet you."

"You told them about me?"

She stopped and nodded. "I told them everything. I hope that's okay." She was cute when she was nervous.

I smiled and shrugged. "Whatever you need."

She gave me another quick hug. *Thanks for not being mad.*

I hated that she thought I'd be mad. I mean, I knew they were humans, but she said they already knew about our kind. And I got that she needed someone to talk to. I wish it was me, but I was glad she at least had someone.

The front foyer was nearly as big as my parents' house. It had two sweeping staircases to the upstairs and looked like something out of a movie. I couldn't believe this was where she grew up. We wound through an enormous living room. There must have been ten couches in there. Plus a library, an office, a ballroom. Each room was more intimidating than the next.

Ember had told me who her mother was, but until this moment I really didn't get it. She was like crazy rich and I could never provide all of this for her. I realized I'd been wrong about coming here.

"Relax," she said. "They're just regular people."

I stared at her like she had two heads. Alicia Kenston was not just some regular person. As we walked into the kitchen, my initial shock told me maybe I was wrong. The Hollywood diva was right there in a pair of yoga pants with a big sloppy shirt. Her hair thrown up in a messy bun. Her husband stood beside her, holding her hand. He truly did look excited. They were nothing like I had pictured.

"Mom, Dad, this is Chad," Ember said. "Chad, these are my parents, Alicia and Martin."

I stepped forward and shook their hands. "It's nice to meet you," I managed to say. I had met tons of parents in my mother's plot to find me a nice squirrel shifter, but they had never meant anything to me. I wanted to make a good impression this time.

"We were just finishing up lunch," her mother said. "Have you eaten?"

"I'm fine, thank you," I said, praying my stomach didn't growl.

Ember turned to look at me and frowned. "He's starving. Do we have any of the broccoli alfredo left?"

"Coming right up," Martin said.

We sat at the kitchen table. It wasn't huge, not nearly as big as my family's, but it was perfect for the four of us and nowhere near as intimidating as the rest of the house. Her parents were funny and helped me relax. It was so surreal though and I kept having to remind myself this wasn't a dream.

After we finished lunch, her parents excused themselves, saying they had plans since they hadn't expected Ember to be home for another day. I wasn't sure if it was true or they were just trying to give us some space, but they disappeared then came back looking more like a Hollywood A-list couple. Alicia hugged Ember and kissed the top of her head.

"Chad, will you be around for dinner?" Martin asked.

"I don't know, sir. I do need to get home to my family at some point today," I admitted.

"Well, I hope you're here when we return, but if not, Happy Thanksgiving and know you are welcome here anytime."

"Thank you, sir," I said, shaking his hand before they left.

I turned my full focus to Ember the second they were out of the room.

"Oh my gosh, they're so cute together," her mother squealed within earshot.

Ember blushed and covered her face in her hands.

"They seem really nice," I said.

She peeked through her fingers at me. "Sorry about all that. I've not brought a guy around here in a long time. They can be a bit much. Usually takes people a few minutes to compose themselves after being around Mom."

"I'm good," I said, and I meant it. What I needed desperately to know was where Ember and I stood.

"We're good too, I think. At least I am. I'm sorry I ran out on you the way I did. The other night, it was. . ."

I cut her off. "Too fast. Too much. I'm sorry. I shouldn't have rushed you."

"No, it wasn't that," she insisted. "It honestly wasn't. You were incredible. I don't regret what happened, not at all. I just sort of went into emotional overload. It was a lot. This whole bonding, mating, whatever we call it thing is a lot."

"So, we're okay?" I asked.

She closed the gap between us, running her hands up my arms as chills shot down my spine. She cradled my face and kissed me. I was stunned at first, but my desperation to claim my mate quickly took over as I returned her kiss, not holding anything back.

Breathlessly she pulled back and rested her forehead against mine. "I fear you may be stuck with me," she said.

I sensed her insecurity. Was she worried about being mated to me, or did she think that wasn't what I wanted? I knew I had sent plenty of mixed signals. First, I'd tried to put her in the friend zone, worrying about what my parents would think but selfishly needing to get to know her. Then, I basically seduced her even knowing she'd had a couple of drinks and might not be thinking straight. It was time to be honest and set things straight.

"Ember, look," I started and watched her face fall with disappointment. "I haven't been fair to you, and I need to be honest. I want you as my mate. I want to be stuck with you for a very long time. I don't want to deny our bond, but I do want to explore it, and then maybe consider sealing it, down the road when you're ready. I've been trying to give you space and let you adjust. I hate that this happened before you even knew it was a possibility. I hate that for you. I don't mind talking about it or telling you what's happening, but I hate that it all overwhelmed you so much. If you want to walk away and break our bond, I'll understand, but that is not what I want."

She shook her head and my heart dropped. "That's not what I want at all. I want you, Chad," she said. "It's crazy, I know, but it's been one week since we met, and I already can't imagine my life without you in it."

My heart swelled with happiness and I kissed her, trying to show her just how much I cared about her and how committed I was to this relationship.

"Mine," I said as I slowly pulled back.

I watched her pupils dilate in recognition and she smiled, happiness filling our bond. "Yours," she said. Then she blushed. "My parents will be gone for a few hours, and we do have the place to ourselves."

Through the bond I saw images of the two of us naked in bed. I grinned, loving where her mind was at. "Lead the way," I said.

She took my hand and we walked back to the front of the house and up the stairs. The room she took me to was huge and very much Ember. There were books everywhere, and the walls were adorned with posters of movies I knew she loved.

"This is much more you than your dorm room," I commented.

She laughed. "Magenta decorated our room. She said my movie posters were tacky and made me take them down." She gave a sour look just mentioning her roommate.

I frowned. I really couldn't stand Magenta.

"It doesn't matter, it's only a few more weeks and I'm moving out anyway."

"What?" I asked, surprised by her declaration.

"Well, I hope that's how it works out at least. My friend Melissa told me her roommate is considering not returning after Christmas break. I hate to say I hope she doesn't, but if that happens, I'm going to move into Melissa's room. I just can't stand it anymore. I can't live with her and her bullshit."

"Things got worse after I kissed you in front of her, didn't they?" she didn't have to say it for me to understand.

She nodded. "It's my problem, I'll deal with her when I get back."

"You don't have to do that alone," I told her. "You aren't alone, Ember."

"I know," she said. "But I don't need you to fight my battles for me."

"What? I can't be your knight in shining armor?" I teased.

She laughed. "You already are."

I kissed her again but didn't let it escalate just yet.

"You know, Damon already moved out. I hate to see him go, but at least for the rest of this semester, I won't have a roommate." She gave me a slightly confused look. "You can stay over anytime you need a place to escape," I told her.

She scrunched up her nose which made her forehead crinkle in that cute way she did when she was weirded out but considering something anyway.

"Wouldn't that be weird? I mean you live in an all guys house," she said.

"Please, the other guys have girls stay over all the time. It's not a big deal," he said.

"It would be to me," she said honestly.

I nodded. "It would mean a lot to me too. I'm not pressuring you, I'm just saying you do have options."

"I'll consider that," she said. "What other options do I have?" she asked coyly.

The atmosphere instantly changed, and this time when I kissed her I didn't hold back. Making love to my girl was going to quickly become my favorite thing in the world. I was still glad I waited, because I knew it could never be the same with anyone else. Ember was mine and I was hers. The thought alone made my two front teeth protrude. She gasped and pulled back, eyes wide as she stared at me. I chose to ignore it and continued on my mission to make us both feel as good as possible.

Someday soon, I thought as she fell apart in my arms.

I curled her up next to me and drifted off to sleep. I stroked her hair and let myself think about our future for the first time. I'd been torn between two majors and knew I needed to commit to one. It wasn't just me I had to think about. I had a mate now, and I'd spend the rest of my life caring for her in every way possible.

Ember

Chapter 14

As I stretched and yawned, still naked in my bed with my mate, I couldn't help but smile and also feel a little guilty about crashing out on him.

"Sorry," I said in a sleepy voice. "I haven't slept well since I freaked out and left you," I confessed. "Last night was more like I wore myself out then passed out.'

"It's okay, you needed it," he said but I could feel he wasn't quite happy.

"What's wrong?" I asked.

"Nothing's wrong. I just really am going to have to head home soon. Mom's called like three times in the last hour."

"Why didn't you just answer it?"

He shrugged.

"Oh, you don't want her to know where you are," she said.

"It's not like that," he tried to say, but I cut him off.

"I know. I'm not a squirrel shifter, but I am. . ." He cut me off this time.

"No, stop that. I know it may bother her, but it doesn't bother me. I don't care what you are Ember. You're mine, and that's all that matters."

I sighed. It was almost like he didn't want to know what my spirit animal was. He always cut me off when I tried to tell him.

"Hey," I said, deciding to change the subject. "Were you close to shifting while we were having sex? I mean I felt your teeth change. Mine also started to change. What was that all about?"

He blushed furiously.

"Are you blushing? Oh, this is something big I'm supposed to know already, isn't it?" I asked, feeling horrible for putting him on the spot and I didn't even know why.

He smiled. "Ember, you can ask me absolutely anything, but yeah, that was something most shifters by our age would know about and understand."

"I'm sorry. I can go back and ask Melissa, or Jenna and Karis said I could call them anytime I had questions."

It wasn't my fault I was raised by humans who didn't know to prepare me for all of this. It wasn't Chad's responsibility to educate me on shifter mating 101 either.

He kissed my forehead and I relaxed against his chest, tracing the planes of his abs with my finger. He groaned.

"I'm never going to get out of here if you keep that up," he said in a deep husky voice.

"Good, that's the plan," I said evilly.

"Ember," he groaned.

"I know." I sighed. "You really do have to go."

"It's only a little over an hour drive. You could come with me."

I looked up at him and I wasn't sure who was more surprised by his invitation.

"I'm sure your mom would freak out with a last-minute guest."

He shrugged. "Maybe, but I could call and ask."

"You really want me to meet your mother?" I shrieked feeling the pressure of such a profound moment. He didn't have to spell it out for me to get the picture that he was a total mama's boy.

"It's not that big a deal," he said, trying to brush it off, but I could feel his nerves.

"Maybe not to you, but from everything you've told me, it will be a very big deal to her," I said.

"I didn't even ask if I could meet your parents. I just showed up on your doorstep and you didn't freak out this badly," he pointed out.

"That's different. They already knew about you and I knew they were excited to meet you." How could he not see the difference? I'd be willing to bet he hadn't even told her about me yet. "Does she know about me?"

He gritted his teeth knowing I was right. "No, but. . ."

"There's no but, Chad. You can't just spring me on her like that."

He leaned over the bed and grabbed his jeans, pulling his cell phone out of his pocket. He gave me a triumphant "watch me" look before dialing a number, even though I shook my head and tried to tell him it was a bad idea.

"Chad? Is that you? Are you okay?" I heard his mother answer frantically. I knew this wasn't going to go well.

"Mom, I'm fine," he said, sounding a little irritated.

"Oh thank God. I thought you said Damon and Karis had an early flight. We expected you hours ago. I've been going sick out of my mind," she fussed.

He rolled his eyes. "And you didn't think to call even once?" he teased knowing she had called numerous times already.

"I did call, and you didn't answer. I figured if you were capable of calling I would have heard from you already." He cringed with guilt.

"Sorry, Mom. I had something I had to do first." He looked down and waggled his eyebrows at me. I playfully punched him in the side making him laugh.

"Chad, this is not funny. I was honestly worried," his mother went on.

"I said I was sorry. This was important."

"And what's so important that you had to make me fret so badly?" she insisted.

"I had to make up with my mate. I couldn't go all week without knowing if she was okay. And I'm fine. I'm still about an hour away, but I will be home tonight," he said so casually I wondered if the poor woman even caught what he was trying to say.

I shook my head at him. *You're really bad at this.*

Chad laughed out loud.

"What is so funny?" his mother demanded.

"Nothing, sorry," he said giving me a look that said I should behave.

"So where exactly are you?" she asked. "You're not talking and driving, are you? You know how nervous that makes me."

"Mom, I'm fine. I'm not driving. I'm at Ember's house. I told you I will be home tonight."

The other line went quiet. "Ember? Who's Ember?"

"You really didn't listen to a word I said, did you?" he teased her.

She was quiet, and I could just imagine she was replaying their entire conversation in her head. She squealed as his words finally registered. "A mate? You have a mate? When? How? Who is she? What is she like? Are you bringing her home for Thanksgiving?"

He chuckled. "Mom, slow down. That's what we're trying to figure out. I'd like to bring her home to meet everyone tonight. Is that okay with you?"

"Okay? My baby boy calls and tells me he's bringing his mate home? Nothing will make me happier."

"She needs to be home tomorrow. She has plans in the afternoon with her mom."

"So you won't be here for Thanksgiving?" she pouted.

"Mom, of course I'll be there for Thanksgiving. Ember's family has their own celebration."

"And what? You're not invited?"

I loved how open and honest his mother was, even though I could feel his irritation. It made me giggle. He shook his head at me, but grinned.

Of course you can stay for Thanksgiving here, I just knew it was a really big deal for your family and it's a pretty quiet family dinner for us. Aside from pulling out the good china and having way too much food, it's not much different than any other meal.

"Mom, I'm invited, I just know how important the holidays are for you and I haven't been home in a while," he reminded her.

"Well what time do they eat? If you're there and only a little over an hour drive, maybe you could do both," she said.

He gave a funny look, seemed to consider it and then concluded that it might be a possibility. I didn't need the bond connection to know what he was thinking. It was clearly written all over his face.

"What do you think? What time do you usually eat Thanksgiving?" he asked.

I shrugged. "Six, maybe seven. I'll text Mom to be sure."

I jumped out of bed and found my jeans to obtain my cell phone. When I stood up triumphantly, I caught Chad staring at me.

Damn, he thought, making me blush.

I shot him a look and pointed to the phone. He shrugged and pulled back the covers to show me just how hard he'd become watching me. I shook my head. No way were we fooling around while his mother was on the phone.

I texted my mom and she quickly replied six-thirty.

I laughed. "I guess split the difference. She said six-thirty."

"That will be a lot of driving back and forth, but if she's important to you then you do it. We'll be eating around one. There's no reason you can't bring her."

"You up for that?" he asked me.

I bit my lip, still nervous about meeting his family, especially his mother, but I nodded. I shot Mom a quick text back telling her Chad would be joining us. I also asked if we could go shopping on Friday or Saturday instead. It took a little explaining, but she agreed. I told her I loved her, and I'd see her on Thursday.

"We rescheduled shopping till this weekend. It will save on some of the back and forth driving, if you think that works?" I said.

Chad considered that. "Okay, hey, Mom, how about if we come home tonight, and you'll have us until after Thanksgiving dinner on Thursday, but we'll spend the rest of the week with her parents instead of wasting time driving back and forth all week. Would that be okay with you?"

"That is a good compromise, son. Now that you have a mate, you're going to have to make all sorts of compromises. I can't wait to meet her."

They said goodbye, but before he could hang up the phone I heard her yelling. "Manny, get the kids moving. This place needs to be spotless. Chad's bringing home a girl!"

He shook his head. "Sorry about that."

"We're really doing this?" I asked.

"Looks like it."

"You're sure you wouldn't rather spend the whole week with your family?"

"I'm positive. You are my family now, Ember," he said as he turned to let his legs hang over the side of the bed as he reached out and pulled me to him.

I leaned down and kissed him. Everything was falling into place perfectly. It wasn't long before our kissing deepened. God could Chad kiss. His tongue teased mine, and a fire ignited inside me.

I loved the feel of his hands on my skin. They were strong and powerful, but his touch was soft and loving. He cupped my breasts, one in each hand. It felt so good. He toyed with my nipples until I couldn't take it anymore. I broke our kiss and threw my head back in a loud moan.

He grinned and slid back on the bed. I pouted until he crooked his finger motioning for me to follow. I slowly climbed up the length of his body and settled over him. Positioning myself just right, I slid onto him. He gave a primal grunt as I began to move. His hands continued to play with me in all my most sensitive places.

I'd had sex before, but every time with Chad was so much more—more intense, more amazing, more everything. The bond between us truly brought us closer. There was no doubt what he needed or wanted, and vice versa. We communicated vocally and telepathically, and it took things to a whole new level of intimacy.

I'm so close, come for me Ember, he said triggering an orgasm of epic proportions.

I collapsed onto his chest gasping for air. My muscles were still spasming and my heart was soaring. Reality hit me hard. I was falling unquestionably and inescapably in love with my mate. I shut down the bond just in time to keep that revelation to myself.

He wrapped me up in his arms where I felt safe and confident. He kissed me until both our hearts began to slow.

The security unit on the wall of my room chimed letting me know my parents were home.

"Ember, we're back," my mom said through the intercom speaker.

"Shit," Chad whispered as he spastically scrambled to find his clothes strewn across my bedroom floor. I sat there laughing at the scene, but as he threw pieces of my own at me, while he came across them in his quest, I dressed, too.

Fully clothed he collapsed back onto my bed with a groan. Looking up at me he sighed.

"Go fix your hair, it looks. . ."

"Like I just had the best sex of my life?" I finished for him.

He grinned from ear to ear. "Damn right."

I leaned down and gave him a quick kiss before heading to the bathroom. I looked in the mirror. My hair was tangled, my lips were swollen, and I had red patches that were not quite hickeys in several places along my neck. He was right.

I quickly scrubbed my face clean and applied my makeup. I glanced back into my room and saw Chad making the bed. He was sweet and considerate, too. I pressed my hand to my heart and sighed.

Deciding to change I went to my closet and opened the door. When I disappeared, Chad came looking for me.

"Holy shit, what is this place?"

I laughed, looking around, trying to see it through his eyes. "It's called a closet. Don't tell me you don't have those where you come from," I teased.

"Ember, you could fit half my house in this room. This is insane. Look at all these clothes. They aren't even flannel."

I laughed. "That's a new obsession." I shrugged. "My mom really likes to shop. I don't bring a lot of name brand labels to school, but that doesn't mean I don't need them when I'm home. I still have red carpet events I'm expected to attend and balls and all sorts of things. Just going to get coffee with Mom can become front page news."

"It's like you have this whole other life. It's hard to connect you in this setting, with the you I already know. Why do you hide all this from people at school?"

"Because I'd never know if they liked me for me, or only for all of this," I said sadly.

He pulled me into his arms. "Luckily for me, you have a personal link straight to my heart and always know what I feel and think about something."

"It does come in handy," I teased.

"And I like you for you, whether that's in jeans and flannels or this." He pulled out a blue formal dress from the rack. "Is that Prada?" he asked.

I laughed. "See, no big deal, right? And seriously, how do you know Prada?"

He smiled. "My sister has a huge label obsession. She wants to be a fashion designer."

"Hey, if she's any good, I happen to know a few people," I offered.

He scowled and shook his head. "I won't let her use you like that."

"It's not using me if I offer, Chad."

I finished getting dressed and grabbed a bag to pack while we chatted. He told me more about his sister, Carolyn, the one who wanted to be a fashion designer. I threw in a few extra outfits I knew I wouldn't wear again that I thought maybe she'd like, but I didn't mention it to Chad.

As he talked animatedly about his family, I learned that all thirteen kids' names started with the letter C.

"You're not planning to continue that tradition with your kids, are you?" I teased.

He laughed. "I guess that's up to you."

I stopped and stared at him, letting that thought sink in. I think it freaked me out more that I wasn't scared by that thought, not one bit.

Chad

Chapter 15

We said goodbye to Ember's parents and headed out. We decided to take her car instead of Damon's simply because it got much better gas mileage and was more comfortable to travel in.

I was nervous about introducing her to my family, but it was an excited nervous. I wanted them to love her as much as I did. *Love?* I considered that for a moment. Yeah, I was falling in love with Ember. I carefully kept that thought to myself. It was still early on and I didn't want to freak her out more than she'd already been.

I amused her with stories of my family. With so many kids in one household, there was no shortage of those or entertainment. The hour drive flew by and we were soon pulling into the driveway of my family's house.

"Is it weird coming home to this house? I mean you didn't grow up here and really haven't spent that much time here."

I shook my head. "Nah. My mom has a saying, "home is where family is." Whether that's an old oak tree, a small apartment, or a nice house, wherever they are is home." He reached over and squeezed my hand. "Wherever you are, is home."

She leaned in and kissed me. As I pulled back I saw her jump. I turned just in time to see a young boy with his nose pressed up against the window. Cody.

"Yup, it's Chad alright," Cody yelled.

"Wow, check out this car," Christian said as we moved to get out. "This is awesome. Can I drive it?"

"This is Christian," I told her. "And no," I said to my brother. "Maybe when you actually get your license."

"But Chad, I can get my permit next month. I need the practice," he said in an attempt to get his way.

"Not in Ember's car you don't. I'll take you out over Christmas break in Dad's truck if you actually pass your test, though."

"Cool," Christian said, giving me a hug

Cody looked up at me. "I lost another tooth, Chad."

"Way to go, Cody," I said, high-fiving him.

I made my way around the car where Ember was still standing, frozen by the door. I reached out and linked our fingers together. I noticed my touch instantly calmed her nerves.

They can be a bit much, but they're harmless, I promise. Everyone's excited to meet you.

As an only child, I feel like I just walked into a foreign country.

I laughed. "Sort of."

"Sort of what?" Cody asked.

"Wouldn't you like to know," I teased as he climbed up into the bed of my dad's truck. I knew what was coming next, but Ember squealed as Cody leapt through the air and landed on my back. I caught him easily. "You'll get used to the chaos," I assured her, though after seeing her house, I hoped it wasn't just wishful thinking.

Still holding her hand, I led her into the house. We passed several of my siblings who all seemed to be on their best behavior. We didn't get attacked by anyone else, but they each said hello as we walked by. I headed straight to the back of the house where I knew I'd find Mom in the kitchen.

"There's my boy," Mom said as she walked over and took my face in her hands. "Let me look at you." She carefully scrutinized me. "You look good, Chaddy. Mating suits you," she said, kissing my cheek before turning her full attention to Ember.

"You must be Amber," she said.

"Ember, Mom," I corrected.

Ember shrugged. "I get that a lot."

"Ember. That's a unique and beautiful name."

"Thanks. You have a beautiful home and a lovely family," Ember said.

"Well, thank you. I'm very proud of this big crazy family, but no need for formalities around here," Mom said as she hugged Ember.

She had to let go of my hand to hug her back, but her apprehension seemed to have subsided some.

"Everyone's home this evening, but you'll have some peace and quiet tomorrow with most of the kids in school. Do you have siblings, Ember?" she asked, not wasting any time to dive right into her life.

"No, I'm afraid not. Only child," she said without going into details. "But I always wished I had siblings."

Mom laughed. "Careful what you wish for next time. I have thirteen precious babies. Chaddy here is my oldest."

"Mom," I warned.

"What? Can't a mother be proud of her first born?"

Ember giggled.

"I'm finishing up dinner now. Why don't you take Ember around and introduce her to everyone? We're having stir-fry for dinner. I hope that's okay. There's a little meat for those who want it, but the majority of us eat mostly vegetarian," she said.

Ember smiled. "Perfect. I do eat meat, but rarely."

When we were safely in the other room I sighed. "Well, that wasn't too bad I hope."

"She's sweet. I like your mom," she said, making me beam with pride.

Carolyn and Crystal walked into the room.

Crystal rolled her eyes. "So, the rumors are true, you found a mate. Didn't think anyone in their right mind would have you."

I hugged her and tickled her while she was in my arms. "What was that? Huh? I couldn't hear you," I said as I continued to torture her.

"Stop picking on your sister, Chad," Mom yelled from the other room.

I shook my head and backed off. "Crystal, Carolyn, this is. . ."

"Emmy Kenston," Carolyn said, then shook her head. "Sorry, I know that's crazy, right? But take off the glasses and glam up the clothes and you could be her twin."

I looked to Ember for how to proceed, but she just smiled. "You must be Carolyn. Chad warned me you were a bit of a fashion expert. I am Emmy Kenston. Though I go by my full name, Ember. You have a good eye. Most people don't recognize me at all outside of the Hollywood scene."

Carolyn's jaw nearly hit the floor. "You're kidding me, right?" She looked around like she expected one of the boys to jump out and yell "Gotcha!".

I shook my head. "She's actually not kidding, Care."

Carolyn let out a loud squeal and I thought for a moment she was going to pass out. "You're serious? You're Emmy Kenston? That means, oh my gosh, Alicia Kenston is a shifter?"

I saw Ember's face drop and thanks to Carolyn's outburst, several of my other siblings started coming in to see what all the commotion was about.

Ember shook her head. "No, I'm afraid not. My parents are human. I was adopted as an infant."

Carolyn's entire attitude changed instantly. She went from the starstruck, Hollywood elite obsessed to the caring and loving sister I adored. "I'm so sorry. I didn't know. Wow, that must have been really hard. Did you know what you were? I mean before you shifted for the first time?"

Ember shook her head again. "Nope. It was almost the biggest shock of my life."

"Almost? What on earth could be more shocking than that?" she asked.

Ember turned to me and grinned, then pointed at me. "This guy talking in my head."

"You're true mates? Chad, you really found your one true mate?" Carolyn asked.

I nodded, possessively putting my arm around Ember's waist. "I did."

"And she's Ember freaking Kenston? That's so cool!"

"Who's Ember Kenston?" Cammie asked.

"Do you remember that movie I took you to where the princess was rescued by that kickass awesome CIA chick?" Carolyn asked.

Cammie nodded. "Oh yeah, that was a great one."

"Well the kickass woman in that movie is Ember's mom."

"No way. That's so cool. Is she that awesome in real life?" Cammie asked.

Ember laughed. "Even cooler!"

My sisters were immediately taken by Ember. They hung onto her every word. The boys came and said hello, curious to meet her, but in the end the majority just brushed her off as yet another sister and went on about their business.

Overall, Ember fit in seamlessly and everyone seemed to love her as much as I did.

Dinner was crazy and normal, well to me at least. Ember had settled in and didn't seem as overwhelmed. Everything was perfect. Carolyn asked if Ember would look over some of her designs. Of course she said yes. Most of the girls snuck off down the hall with them to avoid doing dishes. Apparently it was boys night for that anyway. My brothers cleared the table while I started rinsing and loading the dishwasher.

Mom came in and sat on a stool watching me.

"She's good for you, Chaddy," Mom said.

"Mom," I said, embarrassed.

"No, really. I like her a lot. And to think you found a good squirrel shifter mate without your old Mom interfering. I'm proud of you."

I cringed, and my hands stilled. I took a deep breath and turned to her. "Mom, Ember's not a squirrel."

"What?" she asked like she couldn't believe what I just told her. "She's your true mate. Of course she is."

"No Mom, she's not. I'm sorry if that bothers you, but it doesn't bother me," I said firmly.

Mom sucked in a sharp breath and gave that look that always made me want to run and hide, but I stood my ground.

"Not a squirrel? Ember is not a squirrel? What is she then?" Mom demanded.

I shrugged. "Honestly, Mom, I don't know. I know she's not a squirrel, and I don't care what her animal spirit is. She's my mate," I said firmly.

"Don't care? What do you mean you don't care? She could be an elephant for all you know. It matters Chaddy. That's why you haven't gotten up the courage to ask her, isn't it?" Mom accused.

She physically tilted my head to examine my neck for any signs of our bond mark. Of course there wasn't one because we hadn't sealed it yet. Mom sighed like she was relieved.

"Mom, it doesn't matter that it hasn't happened yet. It's going to happen. I'm sorry if that disappoints you, but she's my one true mate and I would give up anything for her."

Mom knew how much family meant to me, and my words hit her hard. In that moment I knew it was true. I would walk away from all of them if that's what it came to. Ember was my family and the most important person in my life.

Mom started to cry. Dad walked in and shot me a look of disappointment. "What's going on? Why is your mother crying?"

I sighed. "She's upset that I'm mating Ember."

"Why? She seems like a good girl. I thought we liked her," Dad said, confused.

"Yeah, I thought so too," I said with disgust, threw down the dishrag and left the room.

I was pissed. It didn't take long before Ember came to find me sensing my anger. She didn't hesitate when she walked right up to me and placed her hands on my chest. That small contact brought me comfort. It was yet another sign of how our bond was strengthening.

"Are you okay?" she asked sounding very concerned.

"I'll be alright. Want to go for a drive?" I asked her.

"Sure," she said without hesitation.

Carolyn, Christian, and Charlie followed us out to the car.

"I'm not in the mood, you guys. We'll be back in a little while," I warned.

Charlie clapped me on the shoulder. "We're coming with you."

"Yeah, we think Mom's wrong on this, big time," Christian said.

"It's total bullshit," Carolyn added.

"Carolyn," I scolded.

She rolled her eyes and the three of them climbed into the backseat of the Jag. I huffed in frustration. I was trying to get us away from my family, not take them with us.

Are you okay? Ember asked, giving my hand a little squeeze.

No, but I will be, I assured her. *Just need to cool off.*

We knew it would upset her, Ember said sadly. *I just don't get it, I mean isn't it close enough?*

What?

You, me. I mean we're not that different, she said.

We were still talking through the bond when I opened the door and she settled into the passenger seat. Closing the door, I couldn't help but wonder what her spirit animal was. I had been so adamant that it didn't matter that I'd never let her tell me.

As I walked around and slid into the driver's seat, I didn't get a chance to ask her before Christian started talking.

"Chad, can we go for a run? Remember that place you found for us this summer?"

"Is it safe?" Ember asked.

"Yeah, it's a nature preserve," Charlie added.

"Oh yeah, that was cool. Let's do it. I haven't let my squirrel out in far too long," Carolyn added.

I shrugged. "Sounds like fun."

"You aren't an elephant, right Ember?" Christian asked seriously. He looked a little freaked out. Obviously they'd all been listening in on my conversation with Mom.

"No," she laughed. "Significantly smaller than that."

"Big enough to eat us?" Charlie asked.

She really laughed that time. "Um, no, not even close."

"Good enough for me," Carolyn added. "Are you going to tell us or let us be surprised?"

She looked at me like she was studying me. "Do you want to know now? Every time I try to tell you, you shut me down," she pointed out.

"Nope," I said quickly. "Do you want to go for a run?"

Ember shrugged. "Sure, it really does sound like fun."

"Then I suppose I'll see for myself soon enough. And honestly it doesn't matter to me what you are. You're mine. Period," I said. Possession flared within me. *Mine.*

"You better seal that bond soon, Ember. He is not acting right. Chad is always fun and easy going. Nothing bothers him. You must have him all tied up in knots."

"Does sealing the bond help that?" she asked.

Carolyn laughed. "You're kidding right?"

She looked back at my sister seriously and shook her head. "My parents are humans, remember? I'm still learning about all this kind of stuff."

"Oh shit, she's serious," Charlie said.

I glared at him through the rearview mirror. There was an awkward silence for the remainder of the drive.

I pulled into the park and we all got out. There were only a few cars in the parking lot. The basketball and tennis courts were lighted and stayed open late. The nature preserve butted up to it, making it the perfect place to park after dark.

I looked around and was certain no one was watching, then one by one we walked into the woods. Ember and I were the last and I took her hand knowing she didn't know the area. I was sure we looked like lovers sneaking off for a few minutes alone. It wasn't far from the truth, or it wouldn't be if my siblings hadn't decided to tag along.

The boys were already stripped down to their boxers, ready to shift. That possessive thing flared in me again and I moved Ember behind a tree to cover her as I stared down my brothers while she shifted.

My heart was racing as I had no idea what to expect, but when I turned back I couldn't see anything.

Ember? I asked reaching out through our bond.

I'm here, she assured me.

Where? I can't see you, I said starting to panic.

"So what is she?" Christian asked.

Down here, she said. *I'm a chipmunk.*

"Is that her?" Carolyn asked.

I slowly nodded as they stared in shock.

"She is a squirrel," Charlie said.

No, I'm a chipmunk. Do you think that's close enough? Ember asked me.

You're beautiful, but Charlie's right. You're a squirrel, Ember.

No, I'm a chipmunk, she insisted.

"Look at the markings on her back, Chad," Charlie pointed out. "She's an antelope ground squirrel. She thinks she's a chipmunk doesn't she?"

I punched Charlie and told them all to shift and go for their run.

He's right. You're a beautiful squirrel, I said as I stripped out of my clothes and shifted next to her.

My gray squirrel towered over her tiny form. She was the most adorable creature I'd ever seen as she scurried in circles around me.

Ember

Chapter 16

A squirrel? What? I was a squirrel? They must be out of their mind. I looked down at my tiny brown and black arms, then tried to look behind me to verify my white stripes were still there. I caught glimpses of them but felt like a small puppy chasing his tail.

Charlie and Chad both seemed so certain. I would have to look up this antelope ground squirrel and see for myself later. Mom and Dad had only seen me in my fur a few times, but they'd called me a chipmunk. When I looked in the mirror, that's what I'd thought I was seeing, too. Could we have been wrong all these years?

All of his siblings had shifted into gray squirrels like Chad. They looked enormous from my low vantage point. I watched as they took to the trees. I had never really attempted to climb anything. I was more comfortable scurrying across the ground and jumping low lying logs or rocks.

Let's run, Chad suggested. I was positive he felt my confusion.

When I looked over at him, he ran part way up a tree and did a backflip.

Show off!

Chad laughed in my head. *Do you climb?*

Never really had the need or the desire, I confessed.

Go up first. I'm right behind you, he encouraged when we came to a big oak tree.

I gulped when I looked up from the base of it. I didn't want to let him down. If I was a squirrel I must be able to climb trees too, right? Slowly I took one step at a time upwards. My short claws didn't grip deep enough into the bark and I occasionally slid back down. It took me a while, but I did make it up to the first small branch. I perched there to catch my breath.

Looking out I got a little dizzy, but I tried to keep it to myself. Carolyn, Christian, and Charlie were jumping from branch to branch high above us with no fear. Nope, I didn't think that would ever be me.

This doesn't feel right, I finally said. *I want to go back down. Head on up and have fun with them,* I said.

Are you okay? he asked, sounding concerned.

I will be when I'm back on the ground. Charlie did say a ground squirrel. I think that's probably where I belong. Sorry.

Ember, you don't ever have to apologize for being you.

That was probably one of the most powerful statements anyone had ever said to me.

I slid more than climbed back down, and as soon as my feet touched the ground, I was off and running. I knew I hadn't shifted enough while away at college. It was stupid really. I mean, I went to the ARC so that I could learn more about shifters and have the freedom to just be me, but I wasn't comfortable shifting around anyone but my parents. I just didn't shift at school, even knowing there were acres and acres of land to roam risk free.

Scurrying across the ground and jumping from log to log made me reconsider that decision. I had never felt so free running across the forest floor with Chad above leaping from branch to branch with his brothers and sister. I hadn't felt this free since my squirrel broke out and I shifted for the first time.

My life had changed that day in so many ways. I was still dealing with it and wasn't sure I'd ever fully recover from the shock. I wasn't the same person I'd been before that shift. It had made me question everything I knew about life, and I would be eternally grateful for my amazing parents who stuck by me through it all.

We're going to head back now, Chad said through the bond.

I had no idea how long we'd been out there. When I was in chipmunk form, or squirrel from what they were telling me, I lost all track of time. It was only one of the reasons I was hesitant to shift at school.

Okay, I confirmed, slowing my pace to turn around.

I stopped and looked around. Up in the trees above I could no longer see Chad and the others. I stopped and searched my surroundings. I didn't recognize anything. I turned around in a circle trying to get my bearings straight. From down here everything looked so much bigger. And this was reason number two why I didn't shift at school. I had no sense of direction.

You would think there would be some sort of built in animal instinct to help me out, but nope. Maybe mine was broken from being raised in the city with human parents. Maybe I was just born defective. I didn't know. I tried to find something familiar around me, but it was dark, and everything looked the same.

I heard a howl from off in the distance, the hoot of an owl too close for comfort, and then a low growl from somewhere nearby. I couldn't even tell what direction that was coming from and tried not to freak out.

A flash of color through the trees showed me a predator was in the area. I didn't waste time trying to figure out what it was. The first hole I saw at the base of a tree called to me, and I cowered inside as I took shelter from the animal, hoping it would simply pass me by in the night.

As it neared I could hear it more clearly, but I closed my eyes and didn't dare look out. I was as far back against the opposite wall as possible. My heart raced, and I started shaking all over.

Ember? We're back at the parking lot. Where'd you go? Chad asked.

Just hearing his voice calmed my nerves a little until the growling started again, and a shadow passed across the little bit of moonlight filtering into the hole. I held my breath unable to even think or respond to Chad.

Ember? he tried again. *Ember are you okay? Where are you?*

I heard the beast sniff and begin scratching at the hole. In my head, I screamed.

Ember!

D-don't come, Chad. I tried to warn. The snout of the animal poked through the hole. *Coyote! I think it's a coyote. I'm trapped.*

Where?

I don't know. I got turned around. I don't know where I am. I'm in a tree, but he's trying to get to me, I said as tears started streaming down my fury face. I had never been so scared in all my life. I couldn't shift back, sure I'd be bigger than it, but it was a wild animal and I still had nothing to defend myself with. I was entirely helpless.

We're coming. Hold tight. We'll find you, Chad tried to reassure me.

At a time like this, paralyzed by fear as the snarling beast fought to get to me, my life didn't flash before my eyes or anything like that. Instead, as I looked around with no exit or possible chance of survival should the coyote manage to get through and close enough to grab me, a resolution and calm flowed through me.

I had no regrets in my life. Chad could have been one of them, but I'd faced that fear and I knew we would have made it okay. I could have hidden my shifting abilities from my parents and truly been lost in this world, but I hadn't. I trusted them to love me enough despite my differences, and they had. I supposed the only thing I could think of right then and there that I would have liked closure on was Magenta.

My roommate had been a thorn in my side since the day she'd moved in, unannounced. I should have stood up to her. I was a Kenston and had acted like a coward as she walked all over me and issued threats on my life. I made a personal vow that if I survived this, I would fix that as soon as I got back to school. No more!

I was not a coward or a victim. I took another look around. The coyote was still aggressively trying to reach me. There was no way up and no other exits. I was resolved, and I would fight the beast if it came down to it.

In case I didn't survive there was one other thing I needed to do, one last thing I could do.

Chad, I thought, a little too calmly. *If I don't make it out of here, I just want you to know. . .*

He cut me off. *Don't. Don't you dare say it, Ember. I'm coming baby. I just need some sort of sign. Where are you?*

I don't know, I told you that.

I need to hear him. We might be on the right path, but confirmation would help. You said he's a coyote, right?

Yes.

How close are you?

His nose is inside, still about a foot away, but it's right here.

Perfect. I want you to walk up to him and bop him on the nose, he said.

Come again?

I don't know if it's all coyotes, but it's worth a try. Brett's animal spirit is a coyote. The thing he hates more than anything is to be bopped on the nose. Reach out and give that snout a good smack.

You're insane! What if. . .

He won't.

But maybe if I get too. . .

He can't get close enough to you yet. Ember, I need you to try.

I took a deep breath and slowly inched forward. I could feel his hot breath on my fur, smell the putrid remains of his last meal. I pulled my tiny arm back, armed at the ready and I screamed as loud as I could even if it only came out a little squeak. I ran forward, hauled off, and slapped him across the snout with all my might, then I scurried back, out of reach.

The bridge of the coyote's nose cracked against the top of the hole as he pulled back in shock. He disappeared, allowing some light to filter in as I heard him howl in anger.

I heard Chad laughing triumphantly in my head.

Got ya! he said.

Before the coyote could return I heard rustling in the trees above. There was a thud and I heard the beast whimper. Curiosity overruled my fear as I moved to the hole and peeked out.

Nothing could have prepared me for the sight of Chad diving from the branch above and landing on the head of the coyote then using the momentum to shoot back into the air just as two more squirrels came down on his back, repeating a similar acrobatics routine.

The coyote howled in pain and disbelief, running away with his tail tucked between his legs, whimpering the whole way.

Four squirrels landed on the ground before me. Two of them high-fived each other. The largest stepped forward and I ran to him. I knew there were tears in my eyes. I ran around him, letting our tails intertwine.

Come on, let's get out of here in case that guy decides to return. Chad said before telling his siblings to take to the trees and watch out for danger ahead. I didn't know how I knew that's what he was saying, but I did. Their chatter was like an entirely different language, but for the most part I understood it.

Chad stayed on the ground by my side until we were safely back to where we'd left our clothes. I didn't know what I would have done without him.

I quickly shifted and dressed. When the others had too, I ran and hugged the three siblings in one big hug. "Thank you."

They nodded and assured me it wasn't necessary, but I could see the pride and relief on their faces.

I turned to Chad. He didn't give me time to say a word before his lips crushed against mine. I wanted him desperately, right there, despite the possible threat of other animals in the area. But with an audience we kept it PG as I clung to him, feeling safe again and never wanting to let go.

"You guys are cute, but it's getting cold now that the adrenalin is wearing off. Can we go already?" Carolyn complained.

I pulled back and Chad gave me one last quick kiss and kept his arm around me possessively until I was safely back in the car.

"Are you okay, Ember?" Christian asked. It warmed me knowing he was concerned about me.

"Yeah, I am. Thanks so much for your help you guys. I don't know how I would have gotten out of that without you," I said honestly, still a little shaky.

"That's what family's for," Charlie added. "We take care of our own."

My body relaxed with a warm fuzzy feeling. I belonged here. I belonged with these people. I wasn't different, or a freak. Okay, maybe a little, but they got that and welcomed me to their family. Maybe not his mom, but I had to believe she'd come around.

I was free to simply be me, Ember Kenston, socialite and daughter of Alicia and Martin Kenston, closet geek, book nerd, squirrel shifter, future writer, and mate to Chad, and I was ready to fully accept that.

Chad

Chapter 17

When we arrived back home the house was mostly dark. All the younger kids were already in bed and the older kids had adjourned to their rooms likely on their phones texting their friends. Mom was sitting on the couch waiting for us.

"Shit," Charlie whispered.

"Carolyn, Charlie, Christian, head to bed," Mom said.

"Chad, I'd like to speak with you. You too, Ember," she added.

Ember looked at me and I reached for her hand reassuringly. Dad arrived as we sat on the couch adjacent to Mom and took his seat next to her.

"It would seem I owe you both an apology," she started. I was certain my jaw hit the floor. Ember squeezed my hand. "Your father and I talked after you left. Actually, all the kids had plenty to say on the subject. It would seem that I need to step into the twenty-first century. I should have been happy for your happiness. And Ember, I do see how happy you make him and really there's nothing I want more for my Chaddy than that."

Ember laid her head on my shoulder and without thinking I turned and kissed the top of it. I was speechless. Mom didn't apologize for anything. She knew everything, and she let everyone know it. She was opinionated and rarely ever apologized for herself.

"Thank you," Ember said. "That really means a lot to me to hear, but," she started and looked up at me for guidance. I nodded. "But, I may have been wrong." She rushed on to continue. "Chad was so adamant that it didn't matter what I was that he never let me tell him or even show him. All this time I thought I was a chipmunk, and I had thought maybe that would be close enough. But we went for a run tonight, and your children informed me that I'm not a chipmunk after all."

Mom looked confused. "What are you then?

"She's a squirrel, Mom. A beautiful antelope ground squirrel."

To her credit, Mom tried to fight back the grin threatening to spread across her face. The fact that Ember was a squirrel of any kind made my mother immensely happy. It irritated the hell out of me, but I was glad she apologized before we told her.

"Well, it doesn't matter now does it. As long as the two of you make each other happy," Mom said, but the grin she was trying to hide slowly made its appearance.

"Ember, I heard the kids saying your parents are humans?" Dad asked, curiously.

Ember nodded. "Yes sir. I was adopted as an infant."

I could see Dad was bursting with questions. "Do you have any idea where you came from?"

"Well, I know there was a wildfire. I was actually found by a driver in the middle of the fire on the side of the road. That's why my parents named me Ember."

"Like an ember of fire," Mom said.

Ember nodded. "Yup. The driver said a couple of small animals came running out into the road and he swerved so he wouldn't hit them, and there I was just a few feet from the flames. He grabbed me and threw me in the car and got out of there. When it was safe I was dropped off at a local hospital and my parents took me home a few days later. I was maybe a week old by then."

"How old are you?" Dad asked.

"Nineteen, why?"

I could see him doing the math in his head. Something registered on his face and he turned to look at Mom. Her hand flew to her mouth.

"Oh, you don't think?" Mom asked.

"Look at her, it's possible," he said.

Mom stared at Ember and nodded. "Oh my gosh, you could be right."

"What?" Ember asked.

"We remember that fire. We were living on the East Coast and not affected, but we lost many friends that year. It was awful. Martha Turner was pregnant around that time. I think I have a picture somewhere I'll try and hunt up. I'm not saying she's definitely your mother, but it's possible. Martha and Matt would have sacrificed everything to save you if I'm right. That's just the kind of people they were," Mom said.

Ember sat quietly. A single tear ran down her cheek. "You really think that could have been them? I've never let myself think about them."

Mom stared at her for a long time and then nodded. "The more I look at you, the more it's like looking into the past at Martha. I can't believe I didn't see it before."

"I have to ask. Do you know what happened to them? Are they alive?" she asked.

My parents shared a sad look.

"No. I received a birth announcement a week after the fire. I know they had a baby girl, but to the best of my knowledge they were never seen or heard from again."

"Given what I know about that fire, the likelihood that they survived was next to none. My mom and dad are my parents, period. But, you really think you may have known my biological parents?"

"I do. The stories are just too close to be coincidental. There are, of course, tests you could run to confirm, if you decide you want that. I'm still in communication with Martha's mother. Both her parents are alive and well down in San Diego. I would never mention this to them without absolute confirmation. Losing their only daughter was very hard on them both and I couldn't give them false hope."

"I understand. I'll consider it, but I think I need time to really digest all this first."

After another moment passed with Ember lost in her own thoughts that she wasn't sharing, Dad broke the silence. "I'm sorry Ember. That's probably not something we should have just sprung on you like that. We were just taken by surprise is all. It's been a long day. Why don't we call it a night?" he suggested.

I nodded. "Sure. Where do you want Ember to sleep?"

"I kicked the younger boys out of your room for the two of you," Mom said.

I nearly choked, and it took me a moment to recover. "What? You're serious?"

She laughed. "Well she is your mate, is she not?"

"Yes, definitely."

"Despite what you children think, I'm not so old-fashioned as to understand what that means, Chaddy. But if it makes you uncomfortable, she can room in with the girls."

"No, that's not necessary, as long as you're sure you're okay with this?" I asked. It was like my world had somehow been turned upside down. In what universe would my mother be okay with me sleeping with a girl under her roof? She knew we hadn't bonded yet.

Mom laughed and kissed the top of my head as she and dad said goodnight and disappeared down the hall.

"Uh, well, um, okay, let's go to bed," I said feeling super awkward. My parents were right down the hall.

Ember laughed. "The way you're reacting, I'm pretty sure she just guaranteed we are not having sex in this house, huh?"

My face heated, and I couldn't believe I was freaking blushing. I gave her a playful push. "Come on." I took her hand and led her back to my room. It wasn't really mine. The room was the smallest of the four bedrooms. There was a set of bunkbeds for Cody and Cole and then a double bed that Charlie slept on. Under it was a pull-out trundle containing my bed. In our old house, before we moved to the West Coast and I was still living at home, the bed was mine and the trundle was Charlie's. Since I was away at school I told him it was ridiculous to let a good bed go to waste.

Charlie and the twins were crashing in the other boys' room. I felt a little guilty about that. As we entered the room, Ember looked around curiously. I wasn't exaggerating when I'd said her closet was bigger than most of my house, but it was enough for us. I couldn't help but wonder what she saw looking around.

"It's nice. Cozy. I like it here," she said, answering the question I hadn't realized I'd asked.

"Are you okay?" I finally did ask as I looked her over. "My parents can't be one hundred percent certain, you know? About your biological parents."

Ember bit her bottom lip and nodded. "I know. But what they said did make sense. I always assumed they died in that fire. I don't know how to explain it. Maybe it was just that psychological thing of needing the excuse, so I didn't feel they'd just abandoned me. I'm not sure. After I shifted for the first time, Dad and I talked a lot about them. We both agreed that the animals that caused the man to swerve and find me were very likely my parents. But I guess I'll never really know for sure, unless I do a genetic test, I guess. I mean it's possible, but dangerous for our kind. So, yeah, it threw me off a little hearing them, but it really doesn't change anything I didn't already suspect."

I hugged her. I could feel her sadness despite her words.

Someone had already moved our bags into the room. Ember spotted them too and walked over to open hers. I gulped when she stripped out of her clothes without hesitation. I just stood there like an idiot watching her. When the mood in the room changed and she looked slyly over her shoulder, I knew she was well aware I was watching, too.

"Not in my parents' house," I said through gritted teeth. "Put some clothes on, quickly."

She threw her head back and laughed.

"You make me feel like I'm trying to steal your virginity or something."

"You already did that," I pointed out.

She grinned back at me. "True, but right now I really am just getting dressed. It's been a long draining day. You can stop thinking dirty thoughts, because I am exhausted."

We changed and climbed into bed. Ember immediately snuggled up against me using my chest as her pillow. It felt so right to hold her this way. I kissed the top of her head.

Today hadn't gone quite as I'd hoped. In some ways, it was even better. I hadn't imagined when I woke up this morning that I'd be holding my mate tonight, but it was made even more surreal after her near death experience and my realization that I didn't need my mother's approval. Ember was my mate and my future, regardless of whether my family accepted that. I was glad they had, but it had shown me a clear picture of where my priorities were, and what extent I was willing to go through to be with her.

The thing was, ever since I'd admitted to myself my feelings for her, everything had changed. I wasn't just feeling the love of our bond. I loved her. I loved being with her. I loved her quirks, and how humble she was in spite of her lavish upbringing.

Seeing her home and meeting her parents had certainly been eye-opening. I wasn't certain if it had even fully sunk in yet. It was obvious we came from very different worlds, but somehow we still made sense in every way that mattered.

"Chad, can I ask you a stupid question?" Ember said softly, interrupting my thoughts.

I searched her mind and smiled. "That's not a stupid question, Ember," I assured her.

She sat up just enough to look me in the eyes. "I'm nineteen years old, I get how a lot of things work, but I don't understand this bond stuff. I should know this sort of thing and shouldn't have to ask."

"Em, you were raised with humans. They didn't know and couldn't possibly explain everything. You know you can ask me anything, always, right?"

She nodded looking so trusting it made my heart flutter.

"So can you explain it? How do you seal a bond? How is that different from mating?"

"They aren't necessarily exclusive of each other. Just like courting in the human world, it's all a process. We met, the mating signs began. We got to know each other. I guess that's sort of your dating phase. Then the bond began to form. It was sort of there when we first met. We couldn't have heard each other's thoughts without it. Can you feel how it's strengthened?"

She nodded. "Yes. I can feel you now too, your emotions, not just hear your thoughts. I assume that's kind of what you're talking about?"

"Yes. For me, I also feel more protective of you, a need to keep other males away. There's a lightness, happiness that sets in whenever you're around or I hear your voice. And I hated thinking you were upset with me."

"I'm sorry about that. At first I thought you regretted what happened, then I realized you were just reacting to my emotions. You have to admit, all of this happened so fast. It's crazy!"

I smiled. I didn't know exactly when everything had changed for us. She says it was quick and crazy, but to me it was slower than I expected. I wasn't just drawn to her. I wasn't just falling in love with her, but I genuinely liked and respected her because we'd taken those few days to get to know each other as friends first.

I didn't have to say the words aloud for her to understand what I was thinking.

"That's it! When Melissa was talking to me and trying to explain a few things she said something about friendship being the solid foundation of a lifetime together. I've never had a best friend. I could never fully trust anyone to get that close, not with my mom. Too many people used me throughout my life just to get close to her. But with you, I don't have that barrier there. I don't have to hide or pretend. I can just be me and that seems to be enough. I can talk to you about anything. Sometimes I do it without even meaning to, but I do know I can ask you anything, no matter how embarrassing it is. You really have become my best friend, Chad"

I grimaced. "Please tell me you are not sticking me in the friend zone."

She giggled, blushed, then closed the gap between us and kissed me.

"I'm not in the habit of kissing my friends, ma'am," I said sarcastically.

"You better not be in the habit of kissing anyone but me, mister," she responded with more sass than she felt.

I gently kissed her again. "Yes ma'am."

She sighed. *I still need to know about this bond stuff,* she thought.

"Well, stop distracting me then. Like I was saying, first there's the dating stage, getting to know each other and all. Next is where we accept and encourage the bond. I guess, think of it like the engagement stage."

She blushed again. "Uh, how do we accept and encourage the bond? Like how do we move from dating to an engagement in the shifter world?"

She was adorably cute as she faltered on the word "engagement".

I grinned. "Em, we're well into that stage already."

Her eyes widened. "We are?"

She didn't sound horrified by the realization at least, but I couldn't tell if she was actually happy about it.

"Well, yeah. I mean, just being around each other will start to encourage the bond, but um, physical contact encourages it faster. Sex is kind of a given for acceptance."

She gasped. "But that first time. You said you were still a virgin. I thought you were just trying to lose that."

"I was a virgin, and I don't mean to sound cocky, but honestly I had a couple hundred offers to help me lose that card just this year alone." I brushed a loose strand of her hair behind her ear and let my fingers linger against her cheek. "I knew exactly what I was getting into, Ember. I'm only sorry you didn't."

She shook her head. "Don't be. It may have delayed things a little, but I know we'd eventually have ended up right here anyway."

I smiled and kissed her again. I shouldn't have let things go this far without seriously discussing the details and the consequences with her, but I was grateful she was accepting of me anyway. In my heart there was never any doubt. The moment she showed up in my head, I belonged to her.

"Okay," she said a little awkwardly. "So I guess we're sort of engaged or whatever."

I saw a quick flash of a ring in her head and thoughts of a wedding. It wasn't something shifters really did or cared about, though my family was big on celebrating a sealed bond with a big reception like party. Coming from the human world, I couldn't help but wonder if that would be enough.

"Yes we are," I said choosing not to acknowledge the thoughts running through her head. "All that's left is to seal our bond. Which is sort of like the wedding or final vows to each other, I guess. It's so much more than that, though. It's where we tie our souls together for all eternity. There will never be any doubt. There's no such thing as divorce in the shifter world. Once our bond is sealed, I will be forever yours and you will always be mine."

She gulped. We were still young. I got why that would be a lot to take in.

"Ember, it's not something we have to do right away. Just being with you, it's enough right now."

She sighed and was sending off frustration vibes. "Yeah, it's a lot to consider, but it makes sense. The thought of tying myself to anyone at this point in my life should scare the shit out of me, but with you it doesn't. I don't know why, but we'll go with it. I'm more curious about how. How do you seal a bond? Is it something that just happens, like we're accidentally in the engagement period without realizing it sort of thing? Are we going to wake up one day and just know, hey our bond sealed over night? How does it work?"

She wrinkled up her nose at the amusement clearly written across my face.

"You won't accidentally bond yourself to me, Ember. It takes a purposeful exchange of blood to seal the bond."

"Exchange blood?" she said in disgust.

I laughed. "I know it really does sound disgusting. It's all new territory for me too, something I will only ever do with you, but I've been told it's pretty magical. It can sort of start a frenzy of sorts." *Chase swears it'll be the best sex of our lives,* I thought.

"That's a pretty high bar already set," Ember mumbled under her breath causing me to choke and throwing me into a coughing fit.

I couldn't help but grin proudly.

"So how does it work?" she asked again after I'd recovered from her last statement.

I took a deep breath trying to decide how best to explain it. "You know how as a squirrel your teeth change. Our front two teeth elongate, right?"

"Yeah, sure."

"Well, when it's time to seal the bond, your squirrel teeth will surface. We'll use those to bite each other," I said hesitantly.

She cringed but only a little. "Bite each other?"

I held my breath as I confirmed what I'd said and then let it all out at once. "I know it sounds ridiculous, Ember, but I promise you it's a normal shifter thing."

She gave a quizzical look. "Is that even possible? What if it doesn't break the skin?"

I laughed. "Have you ever felt your teeth in squirrel form? Think of all the things we eat, the hard shells we crack using them. Those suckers are razor sharp, you don't need to worry about that."

"So that's it then? You bite me. I bite you. I don't have to suck your blood out or anything do I?" she asked. My face must have given away the answer, because she scrunched up her nose in disgust. "Ew, gross!"

"It's not gross, it's beautiful." I brushed her hair to one side and leaned in close to kiss the spot I knew that I'd one day mark her there. "And when it's done, you'll bear my mark. Right here," I said as I leaned in and kissed her neck once again. This time she shuddered. I ran my hand up her arm, feeling the goosebumps I'd caused to break out across her skin. I pulled back and smiled in satisfaction.

"Does it hurt?"

I shrugged. "From how Damon explained it to me, by that point we'll be so caught up in this sort of euphoria that we likely won't even notice. Our squirrel spirits know what to do and when to do it. It usually happens during a time of intimacy. You'll feel your teeth come in, but you won't be shifting. You'll still be fully you." I really hoped I wasn't explaining this all wrong.

Her eyes went wide again, and she opened her mouth to say something, then shut it and looked at me curiously.

"What?" I asked when I couldn't read her thoughts.

"That happened earlier today. We were making love in my bedroom. I started to freak out, but we were kissing and then I felt yours, too," she confessed.

I grinned and nodded. "Yeah, it did. It's sort of our animal spirits giving us a swift kick in the ass to finish it and seal our bond already. But don't worry, there's no rush. I'd wait for you forever. We'll know when the time's right for us."

Ember

Chapter 18

It was already into the early hours of a new day, so I settled back into position next to Chad and thought through all he'd explained. Some of it sounded crazy, but it resonated as truth. I trusted him, and I was glad he was willing to talk about it so openly. I sensed it was a very private and intimate sort of thing that wasn't discussed a ton. No wonder my dad didn't have a good understanding of what was happening to me.

"Are you okay?" Chad asked, and I knew he was looking for reassurance that I wasn't going to freak out and run away again.

"I'm okay. Just taking it all in, and I'm suddenly very tired. It's been a long day."

He chuckled. "Yeah, you could say that again." He kissed the top of my head. "Sweet dreams Ember. We can talk more in the morning."

"Good night, Chad."

I wanted to tell him I loved him, but the words wouldn't form.

* * * * *

Just like the last time, I woke peacefully in Chad's arms. *I could definitely get used to this,* I thought.

Good. If I get you addicted enough this week, maybe you'll actually consider staying with me when we get back to the ARC, he responded.

"Did you just inadvertently share your diabolical plan with me?" I asked.

Chad laughed. "I guess I did."

I moved off of him and he rolled onto his side to look at me. Before I could even say, "Good morning," he kissed me. I groaned as I pressed my body against his and felt how hard he was.

He pulled back and shut his eyes. I could hear him willing himself to calm down, reminding himself that his mother was just downstairs cooking breakfast. I laughed and pushed to get up.

"In that case, I'm taking a really cold shower," I confessed.

He groaned in frustration, covering his face with the pillow, but still standing at full attention.

"I could take care of that for you," I offered, eliciting a few swear words from under the pillow.

I grabbed my bag and left. I was laughing, but in truth, I wanted him just as badly. Knowing he'd already made it very clear that nothing was going to happen under his mother's roof, I did take a cold shower to try and settle the desire welling up in me.

It was crazy! I felt like a horny teenager struggling to keep my hands off him. I wouldn't turn twenty for another four months, so I supposed that was exactly what I was. I laughed to myself. "Get a grip, Ember," I scolded.

I felt mildly better and ready to face the day, until I walked back into the bedroom to find Chad in only a towel wrapped around his waist with water dripping from his hair.

Are you seriously trying to provoke me to break your, not here rule? I thought to myself.

"Sorry," he said and genuinely looked it. "I thought you'd be longer."

My hair was still wet and thrown up into a messy bun. I was wearing jeans with a navy T-shirt and a yellow and blue flannel wrapped around my waist. Nothing fancy, but he was staring at me like I was the most beautiful woman in the world.

He shook his head. "Sorry. I'll just be a sec."

I plopped down on the bed and stared up at the ceiling, trying hard not to roll over and watch him dress. No good would come from it. But I had only just met his family and wasn't comfortable wandering down to the kitchen without him. I looked up and saw he was fully dressed and looking very handsome. I smiled.

For the first half of the day Chad stayed by my side as I got to really spend time getting to know everyone. Using me as an excuse, their mother caved and gave them all a pass to skip school for the day, as well as the half-day they were scheduled for on Wednesday.

I had never experienced a family dynamic quite like it before. It reminded me of that movie *Cheaper by the Dozen*. I was fascinated by how chaotic it felt to me, yet on closer observation it was the beautiful synchronization throughout the house that drew my attention.

By lunchtime I was feeling more relaxed. I played board games with Cammie and Cassie, the eleven-year-old twins, until Carolyn decided she needed to go shopping. Apparently, she always found an excuse to go shopping. That's when I remembered the extra clothes I'd thrown in for her.

Sizing up Chad's sister, I knew we were close enough in size that the stuff I'd brought should fit her.

"I have another idea, if you want," I suggested.

Their mom looked at me gratefully as if to say, "Thank God. I can't handle anymore shopping with this girl."

I stood up and grabbed Carolyn's hand. "Come on," I said as I dragged her down the hall in the opposite direction of the door.

"Can we come too?" Cassie asked.

"Sure," I said.

Once we were settled into the bedroom with the door closed behind us, I pulled out the extra bag I'd packed and tossed it to Carolyn.

"What's this?"

I shrugged. "Chad told me you were really into fashion. I grabbed a few things I'll likely never wear again. Since we're close to the same size, they should all fit you."

"You're giving her your clothes?" Cammie asked.

I nodded. "I really don't need them and thought you'd like them. It's nothing major, just a few outfits I grabbed at the last minute."

"Carolyn despises hand-me-downs," Cassie warned me.

I grinned. "Something tells me she won't mind these."

Carolyn hesitated, but curiosity got the best of her as she slowly opened the bag. Her jaw popped open as she carefully pulled out the first piece, mesmerized as she gently felt the fabric and assessed the garment with a critical eye.

"This is real," Carolyn said after her assessment. She was in a sort of daze over the clothes, something I would never understand.

"This one still has the tag on it," Cammie added as the younger girls dove into the remainder of the bag's contents.

Carolyn snatched it up. "This is brand new, Ember. And it's this year's line."

I gave a nod. "I'll never wear it. My mom has a bit of a shopping obsession. Oh, she's tried to convert me to her shop-a-holic ways for years, but it's a moot point. You, she'll adore!"

"You're going to introduce her to your mom?" Cassie asked.

"Sure. I hope she gets to meet all of you," I said. Chad had described this stage as our engagement period. Of course I wanted our families to meet.

Carolyn set down the shirt she had been fawning over and frowned. "This is too much Ember. I can't take these."

"Why not? Look at me. I prefer jeans and T-shirts. I've found a love of flannel my mother will never understand. I get to be me at the ARC."

There was a knock at the door, and I knew it was Chad.

"Come in," I yelled.

He came and sat down beside me. He was feeling my frustration that his stubborn sister wasn't going to take the clothes.

"Care, it's okay," he said. "If this was Catherine's stuff you'd snatch it up in a heartbeat and wouldn't think twice."

"But it's not, and Catherine could never afford these things."

"Maybe not now, but you never know what the future holds. If you don't want it, say thanks but no thanks and we'll drop it off at Goodwill on our way to her house tomorrow."

"What?" Carolyn screeched. "You cannot take these to Goodwill. Are you insane?"

I laughed. "Well they aren't coming back home with me. I have way too much stuff as it is."

"She is not kidding. Half this house would fit into her closet."

I rolled my eyes. "It's not that big."

"Ember, there are two couches inside your closet. That's not normal," Chad insisted.

"I want to see it!" Cassie chimed in.

Cole peeked his head into the room. Clearly he'd been listening to everything. "Can we play hide-and-seek in there?"

Chad laughed. "Dude we wouldn't find you for a week in there."

"Cole's really good at that game," Cammie informed me.

"Carolyn, go try something on," Chad encouraged.

"You're positive?" she asked me one last time.

"Yes, now go," I insisted.

She gave a squeal as she snatched up the bag and headed for her room. A couple more trickled in while we waited. Half the family was now crammed into the small bedroom.

Carolyn entered the room with a twirl as everyone clapped. She had mixed and matched a few of the outfits and looked absolutely stunning.

"You really do have a great eye for fashion, Carolyn. I would never have thought to do that."

She made her way over and hugged me. "Thank you, Ember," she said before the girls pulled her away to gush over her.

Chad reached out and squeezed my hand. *Thanks.*

I looked around at all the siblings. They were kind to each other. You could feel the love in the house. It was something I didn't think was real, only found on television fantasy worlds. But here I was witnessing it. Here, I was a part of it.

I would never in a million years have pictured Chad in this environment. It made me see him in a whole new light. I had never given much thought to children and family but looking around I knew this was what I wanted: a big, crazy, loving family of my own.

I didn't mind the peace and comfort of a quieter house. I had never taken issue with being an only child. My parents had always doted on me. My mom was my best friend and I had a wonderful life, but this was even more. I felt complete being surrounded by them all.

The day passed much too quickly and soon day turned to night and the house began to settle. Chad and I retreated back to our room and stayed up talking late into the night.

The next morning I awoke starving. I wasn't just hungry for food; I wanted my mate. Sleeping in his arms each night was amazing, but the physical desire to be even closer to him was hard to ignore. Sexual tension was apparently a real thing. I briefly wondered if I tried to seduce him, would he really say no?

"Are you hungry?" Chad asked, disrupting my thoughts.

"Starving." We both knew I meant in more than one way, but I'd settle for food. As if in agreement, my stomach rumbled.

We laughed as he grabbed my hand and pulled me up from the bed. One quick kiss and we were off to begin an exhaustingly fun day of baking and prepping for Thanksgiving. Chad's mom ran a tight kitchen and employed every single one of her children. She informed me early on that I was no exception to that list.

I had never really done much cooking, but I was able to help chop vegetables and with Carolyn's help I even made a cherry pie. It didn't look like the ones that Mom always had the caterer make for us, but Carolyn seemed optimistic it would taste good even if it was the ugliest pie ever made. Still, I was proud that I did it.

Sixteen hours later I collapsed back into bed completely exhausted. Who knew cooking and family time with a group this size could be so tiring?

The next morning I awoke to delicious smells filling the house. I thought the smells of baking pies had been delightful, but it was nothing compared to the fragrance of actual Thanksgiving.

Mom wasn't much of a cook, and although Dad had tried his own attempt at cooking Thanksgiving when I was young, we'd given up on that years ago and just had it catered. A picture perfect, delicious holiday that suited us all.

This was nothing like Thanksgiving in the Kenston home.

When we walked into the kitchen, his mom immediately motioned us towards the dining room. There was a mountain of muffins in every flavor imaginable piled high on plates.

"Sorry. I hope you like muffins. It's sort of a holiday morning tradition around here," Chad said.

I stared at him like he was crazy. "Are you kidding? This is amazing!"

"Grab what you want before the little ones wake. They go quick around here," his mom said as we sat down. She walked behind Chad and gave him a quick kiss on the top of his head. As she walked past me to head back into the kitchen, she kissed my head too. Chad stopped eating and stared, then smiled. I knew that small gesture had just made him very happy. It made me happy too, like I was really part of this family now.

I offered to help numerous times, but I guess I hadn't been all that impressive in the kitchen for preparations the day before. Instead we headed outside and got a game of volleyball started with everyone who hadn't been assigned kitchen duties.

As if sixteen people wasn't enough for dinner, shortly after noon others started arriving. I had been to a lot of large affairs, but I had never seen so many people crammed into such a small space before. Tables wrapped through the dining room, into the family room, and even into the foyer, but everyone had a seat.

When the last bowl was placed on the table, Manny motioned for everyone to sit, and a hush came over the room. He asked us to bow our heads and then he prayed. My family wasn't exactly religious, so I didn't know what to do. Everyone looked down at their laps, so I did too. As he spoke some beautiful words about blessings and family and friends, I looked around the table noting everyone else's eyes were closed with smiles on their faces.

What were they thinking? What did they feel? I couldn't help but want to analyze it all. I knew that was a part of my father in me. I may not have his blood flowing through my veins, but I definitely had his scientific curiosity.

As Manny ended his prayer with an "Amen," the entire room transformed into noise and mass chaos as the bowls and platters were reached for and passed around. Even after two days of adjusting to their world, I wasn't prepared for Thanksgiving dinner. I sat back and watched, feeling overwhelmed by it all and scared to jump in and grab something even when the sweet potato casserole passed me by. It was my favorite.

Chad jumped right in and began snagging dishes as they flew down the table.

Don't worry, I got you, he told me as he shot me a sly grin and began filling my plate along with his, starting with the sweet potato casserole.

Thank you.

After the initial madness, everyone settled down. The food was delicious, the conversation was pleasant, and soon we were stuffed, miserable, and begging for dessert. I wasn't sure I had ever eaten so much at one time in my entire life. I knew I was going to have to hit the gym everyday till Christmas to get the weight back off, something that was far more difficult in the fall and winter months.

After dinner, we said our goodbyes. I hugged so many people I thought my arms would fall off if I had to hug even one more person, but it had been wonderful, and I wasn't lying when I told them all I couldn't wait to see them again over Christmas break.

Chad

Chapter 19

Ember was quiet as we made the hour drive from my house to hers. I worried that Thanksgiving dinner at my house may have pushed her over the edge.

I reached for her hand, lacing our fingers together. "Are you okay?"

She smiled back at me. "I'm great, though I may need a few days at the spa to recuperate." She laughed. "You may have noticed, I have a bad habit of retreating into myself when I get overwhelmed. I pushed through pretty well this week, I think. It was a lot of fun, but it was a lot more extroverted than I'm used to."

I smiled. "I get it. They're a lot. Last year I headed back to campus on Friday just to sleep the weekend away before facing classes again. And I'm used to them."

She seemed relieved. I wasn't exactly an introvert, but I did understand it. It wasn't so bad when I was there every day and living that life, but once I'd gotten away from my family, visits seemed even more insane. I couldn't imagine what Ember was feeling, but I knew my oldest sister, Catherine was a complete introvert. She was likely locked in her room hiding in her sketch book right about now trying to recover from the extra insanity of the holiday, so I got it.

"It was fun. I'm glad you invited me, but it is very different from my family. Where you guys bring family and friends together for the holidays, with Mom's career we kind of live that party life too much in the everyday, so holidays tend to be quiet affairs with just the three of us. Now four," she added with a smile.

"I'm sorry we stayed so late. I'm sure your mom will want some help in the kitchen getting dinner ready."

Ember snorted. "Mom doesn't cook. Like ever. Her idea of cooking is reheating leftovers, and that can be a challenge sometimes. She cooked Thanksgiving weeks ago I'm sure—cooked as in placed her order with the caterer."

I looked at her, appalled. "You don't cook your own Thanksgiving?"

"Trust me when I say that it's a huge blessing. No one wants to eat my mother's cooking. Any homecooked meals I had growing up, Dad cooked. He's not so great at it either, but props for trying I guess."

"I can't even imagine," I admitted

She rolled her eyes and smiled. "That's because your mother makes Martha Stewart look like a slacker."

I laughed. I knew it was true.

Ember turned on the radio and seemed to relax as we sang along, holding hands for the remainder of the drive.

We were laughing and in good spirits as we pulled into the driveway and walked towards the house. It felt strange not knocking on the front door. Ember just opened it and let us in. I knew it was her house, but it still intimidated the crap out of me.

She walked to a console on the wall and hit a button. "We're home," she said to seemingly no one.

I pulled her into my arms and she giggled as she wrapped her arms around my neck and kissed me. The house was so big I briefly wondered if her parents would even notice if I made love to her right in the middle of the foyer.

Within seconds of thinking that, her dad strolled down the ornate staircase. "Pumpkin!" he said, obviously excited to see her. She unwound herself from me and walked over to hug him. He pulled her back to take a good look. Seeming happy with what he saw, he grinned. "Much better."

"Daddy, please don't make a fuss," Ember warned him. I could see she was blushing.

"Can I see it?" he asked, excitedly.

She scrunched her nose as she did when she was frustrated or confused. "See what?"

"Your bonding mark," he said, causing her to turn ten shades of red darker.

She smacked at him playfully. "Daddy! There's no bond mark to show," she said lowering her voice probably hoping I didn't hear her.

"What? Why not?"

I snorted, surprised by his reaction. Did he really want me to mate his nineteen-year-old daughter?

"Dad, you do realize that's sort of a forever thing, right? Like stronger than marriage even. You really want me to rush into a decision like that?"

I watched for his reaction as he scrunched up his nose in the same way Ember always did. "It's different for your kind. I'm sorry I never properly prepared you for all of this."

Ember crossed her arms over her chest and I could feel her defiance strengthen. If Martin kept talking, I'd be lucky if she ever kissed me again, let alone sealed our bond.

"Have you really thought this through?" she asked him. "I mean I'm grateful that you're willing to accept Chad into our lives without question, or even really taking the time to know him. I'm even happy to hear you understand there's a difference between *our kind*," she said.

"Oh no you did not. Martin Kenston," Alicia started, and I watched the grown man wince. "Tell me you did not tell my baby that she is somehow different from us."

I looked around in the direction both their heads had turned and watched her appear around the corner as if she'd just materialized before us. I could tell this was a very sensitive subject in their family.

"Sweetheart, I was only trying to say that she shouldn't be scared or fight the bond. Yes, it's different, but it's also special."

I watched as Alicia took a deep, calming breath. Holy shit was she scary when she was pissed. "Before we start anything, we're taking this to the living room." They both nodded and turned to head in that direction, or I assumed it was the right direction. The house was so big I could easily get lost in it. "Chad, come along. Although I am mortified by my husband and daughter's outburst in front of company, it would seem in some odd way you are suddenly family. I won't begin to even try to understand it all."

I bit back a grin as I followed her down the hall and through the house until we entered the family room. Ember was already sitting on one couch with her arms still crossed. Martin was the spitting image across from her.

"They don't look alike, and I know they aren't blood related, but it's kind of freaky how alike they are," I confessed to Alicia.

She immediately softened. "It's downright scary sometimes. You have no idea, Chad."

She motioned for me to take a seat next to Ember and she sat beside Martin.

This isn't awkward at all, I thought.

Ember's stance softened, and she turned worried eyes my way. *I'm sorry.*

After all the shit my family put you through? Don't even give it another thought, I told her. By all rights my mom should have scared her off that very first night. She hadn't let that come between us, and I wouldn't let this either. Although I was confused; Martin seemed to be rallying for us, but Ember was being obstinate and seemed determined to argue against us.

She sighed. *It's not like that, exactly.*

Then how exactly is it? I asked before I could stop myself.

"No. Cut it out. All conversations are open and honest in this home. None of that weird telepathy stuff right now. Whatever you need to say should be done so aloud," Alicia insisted.

Martin seemed excited, almost giddy, like he was barely containing himself as he observed us.

"I won't pretend to understand anything about this bonding stuff, but I gather it's serious," Alicia started.

"Mom, it's basically like marrying him, only there's no chance of divorce. Daddy says I shouldn't fight it and doesn't understand why we haven't sealed the bond yet. He's not thinking rationally," Ember said.

"Rationally? This is all science, pumpkin. God, or nature or whatever you choose to believe, created you this way. You were created to find him and spend the rest of your life together. Patrick says it's the greatest thing in the world."

"And your friend, Patrick, he's a squirrel shifter?" she asked.

"No. A wolf actually. He and his mate, Elise are very happy," he said.

My eyes widened with recognition. "Woah, woah, woah. Hold up. Are you talking about Patrick O'Connell and Elise Westin?"

Martin looked surprised but nodded.

I laughed. Of course I knew Patrick. Elise was Chase's sister and I was very familiar with the nightmarish stories of their mating period. "I truly appreciate that you seem to be on my side for this mating, sir, but Patrick and Elise are among the last shifters on Earth that you'd ever want to use as an example. She put him through hell for months and was determined not to bond with him," I blurted out.

"Westin? Is she related to Chase?" Ember asked.

I nodded. "Yeah, Elise is his oldest sister."

"What happened to them?"

I smiled. "They had a really rocky start. She ran away, and then was kidnapped by a rival pack. She fought their bond tooth and nail."

"But they still ended up together and are as happy as two people could possibly be," Martin added. "I didn't know all the details of their mating—oh my poor friend. Then again, we likely would never have met if it weren't for Elise being kidnapped."

My curiosity piqued. "How exactly do you know Patrick and Elise, sir?"

Martin took a deep breath. "Now that is something I'm only ever supposed to discuss with family."

Ember rolled her eyes. "Just because we haven't sealed our bond doesn't make him any less a part of this family, daddy. It's just a matter of time. I'm still learning and adjusting to all of this. Don't rush me. If he were a human and I came home at nineteen and said, hey, we're getting married, you'd probably threaten to kill him. This is bigger than that and I'm still only nineteen, remember?"

I could feel her anxiety swell between the bond. "What are you really worried about Em?" I asked. I really needed to know the answer to that one simple question. I held my breath not sure I wanted the answer, though.

"What are the tabloids going to post?" she asked, blushing feverishly.

Alicia gave her a knowing look and came to sit beside her. Ember rested her head on her mother's shoulder and leaned into her comforting embrace.

"You don't need to be worried about that, sweetie," her mom said gently.

"Yes I do," Ember said adamantly. "It's only a matter of time before they take notice of Chad. They'll ask questions. They always do. They'll look into his family, Mom. That's a risk."

"Ember, honey, that's too much on your shoulders. It's going to be okay. We can simply give a press release at the wedding."

I was glad I hadn't been drinking something, because I would have choked. "The wedding?" I asked. Shifters didn't marry. What was the point? I was going to bond with her. Weddings were ostentatious and unnecessary, plus they cost a lot of money. I didn't have that kind of money.

"Yes, a wedding. It would solve all of your problems," Alicia said.

"No, it wouldn't," Ember said, pulling away from her mom. "That doesn't solve anything at all. I'm nineteen. If I get married, every paparazzi around the globe will be stalking me, looking for a baby bump and you know it. People don't marry at my age unless they're pregnant or attention seekers."

Martin shot me a look and I held my hands up in surrender. "She's not pregnant," I tried to assure him. "We've been careful."

I saw the clench of his jaw before it registered what I'd just said. I quickly shut my mouth and was determined not to open it again.

"Safe is good," her mom said, adding to my discomfort as well as Martin's.

Ember rolled her eyes at them. "Mom, I was fifteen when you put me on the pill and I got my first IUD before entering college. You know I'm not going to get pregnant."

Martin cleared his throat awkwardly. "There are other reasons for protection than just pregnancy, Ember. I realize your k. . ." Alicia turned that look of death on him again and he quickly changed his verbiage. "I mean, I realize that you have a stronger immune system than most people, but that doesn't mean you're entirely protected against common STD's. I'm just saying I think it would be a smart choice if you both got tested is all."

"Oh my gosh. We are not having this conversation, Daddy!" Ember squealed.

"I was a virgin. I'm no threat in that department," I blurted out.

Ember's jaw dropped at my candidness.

"Definitely sticking with team Chad," Martin said without missing a beat.

I can't believe you just told them that.

I can't believe I just told them that!

"I'm so sorry, Mr. and Mrs. Kenston. When I get nervous I sometimes talk a lot and don't necessarily think before speaking," I said.

The three of them burst out laughing and I wanted to shift and hide in Ember's closet knowing they'd never find me there.

I'll always find you, Ember said through the bond.

When I finally turned to look her way, she was smiling happily and some of the tension had lifted.

"What if we just got engaged then?" I said. "I mean regardless of when we seal the bond that doesn't have to matter towards the outward appearance for paparazzi and all, right? If you want to have a wedding down the road, I guess we could consider it."

Shit! What was I saying? A wedding? That was the worst idea ever, I thought.

But you'd do it for me, wouldn't you? Ember said. It was a question, but didn't really sound like one, more like a revelation.

If it means that much to you, I guess I would, I told her honestly.

"I thought we said none of that here," her mother teased. "So, do we have an engagement then?"

Ember shrugged. "I guess I'm okay with that."

Alicia squealed. "I have just the ring. Let me go get it."

I was shaking my head before I could formulate the words. "No. If this is the plan then we're going to do it right. Not here, not tonight, but when we're ready. When I'm ready. It wouldn't be uncommon for us to be dating. We met in college, end of story for now. That's if anyone notices and comments."

"We're having lunch at the Club tomorrow. Trust me, you won't go unnoticed," Alicia informed me.

"But Chad's right. There will be questions, but a simple, "we met in college and are dating" is appropriate and technically correct."

I shot her a look. We'd decided we were already in the engagement phase of human relationships, but I'd just freaked out over a forced engagement, so why did it equally bother me to hear we're just dating now. I was so screwed up and my emotions were all over the place.

When I'm ready to put a ring on your finger, it'll be for real, not for show, I told her, hoping she'd understand where my thoughts were on the subject. *I don't want your mother's ring. I will pick it out myself, one that I can afford, and I'll ask you the right way. It may not be a common shifter thing, but my mother and sisters watch enough Hallmark Movie Channel movies for me to understand this basic human practice.*

Ember dabbed at her dampened eyes and nodded at me. I knew she wasn't upset. My words had made her happy.

"I feel like we're missing entire conversations here. No fair on the mind speaking stuff," her dad complained. "But seriously, is that not the coolest thing ever? What I wouldn't give to experience it just once."

"It's not always great, Dad. I have to monitor my thoughts to keep anything to myself. He's always there. It's not that easy or wonderful. There's no privacy," Ember said.

I had never considered that before. Then again, I knew all about the mating process and what to expect. She hadn't, so of course it would feel more like an invasion than a gift to her. To me it was the most amazing gift ever. I never wanted to hear just my own thoughts again.

"Well, I'm just thankful you're both home. Chad, we look forward to really getting to know you this week. I know her father's a little over zealous and excited about this bonding stuff, but all we truly want is for our baby girl to be happy."

"Amen to that," Martin added.

"Now, dinner is getting cold, so I think we should all adjourn to the dining room," Alicia said.

"Yeah, 'cause we certainly don't want the love of my life trying to heat it back up," Martin added as we rose just in time for Alicia to elbow him in the side.

Ember took my hand and led me further into the house to the dining room. It was like something you'd see in a palace. The room was enormous, and the table could easily have sat my entire family around it with room to spare. On the far end were four place settings, a picture-perfect turkey, and all the fixings in decorative crystal bowls.

It did look like Thanksgiving dinner, just a whole lot fancier than I was used to. Martin and Alicia headed down one side of the table and Ember tugged on my hand to follow her down the other side. No one sat at the head of the table. That was the most bizarre part to me. My father always sat at the head of our table.

Once seated, I noticed that while the turkey looked like a work of perfection, it was mostly decorative and had already been cut and artistically recreated to look like the perfect turkey.

"Everything smells wonderful, dear. You really outdid yourself this year," Martin teased as he and Ember snickered.

"It looks lovely, Mrs. Kenston," I said.

"Please, none of that Mr. and Mrs. crap, Chad. Just Martin and Alicia."

"Yes ma'am. Well, it looks wonderful, Alicia," I corrected.

"Thank you. My cooking skills are legendary, and the stuffing is to die for," she added with a wink.

"Legendary. Right. I've already been warned of that," I said, again opening my mouth before it registered okay with my brain.

Martin had just taken a bite out of a turkey leg and Ember nearly snorted her sparkling cider as they both burst out laughing.

Alicia shot me a look, then smiled brightly and shrugged. "I can't be great at everything," she said good humoredly.

We chatted about lighter topics as we ate. There was surprisingly a lot of laughter and happiness at the table. I wasn't quite sure what I'd expected from the A-list family holiday, but mostly it just felt normal. Then again, I'd always found Ember to be one of the most real and level-headed people I'd ever known, so I supposed I shouldn't be too surprised to find she got that from her parents too.

Ember

Chapter 20

Things had started off awkwardly and embarrassing with my parents, but Chad had taken it all in stride. Dinner had been the best I could ever remember. Mom and Dad even volunteered to clean up afterwards and I'd accepted, saying goodnight early and heading back to my room.

"They won't think we're being rude?" Chad asked in a whisper.

We were on the opposite side of the house and there was no way my parents could hear us. Heck, I wasn't even sure a wolf shifter would be able to from that distance. The gesture made him adorably cute though.

"No, they're fine. Don't worry so much. I'm the loner, remember? They're used to me needing my downtime." It was true. I'd been this way my entire life.

"But you aren't alone, and they know it," he reminded me.

I laughed. "Stop whispering. You make it sound like we're doing something we shouldn't be."

"Aren't we?" he asked.

"I guess that depends on what you had planned for the night. I was thinking a movie," I said.

"A movie?" he asked.

I nodded. I didn't want him to know that I really wanted to just strip his clothes off and straddle him. But he would clearly be on board with that plan, because in his confusion over my movie suggestion he accidentally showed me a picture of him feasting on dessert where I was his chosen sweet treat. Desire consumed me, and my body tingled all over.

"How did you do that?" I asked in wonder, trying to regain some control after such a vivid and erotic image.

"Do what?" he asked heading to the bookshelf next to my TV filled with DVDs.

I pursed my lips and shook my head. "Never mind."

He turned to stare at me, his eyes concealing little of his own desire. "What did I show you?"

I took a deep breath and stared into his eyes. "Dessert. In graphic images," I said.

He stared back taking a sniff of the air. No doubt he smelled my arousal. The DVD he held slipped from his hand and crashed to the floor, but we never broke eye contact as he stalked towards me.

I waited, unmoving. He towered over me as I looked up to maintain eye contact the closer he got. He reached out and gently stroked my cheek with his fingertips.

"So beautiful," he said. "Mine. I need you to understand Ember that I have every intention of spending the rest of my life with you. I know that still terrifies you some, but for me you're it. You're everything, you're the one I waited for and you were definitely worth the wait. Now that I've had you though, I'm not sure I could ever get enough."

His words felt more like gentle caresses and my squirrel shuddered in excitement. *Soon,* I promised her.

When he finally leaned in to kiss me, there was no doubt in my mind that I was his and he was mine and we would spend the rest of our lives together.

Before things got too out of hand he pulled back and cooled things between us.

"How about that movie?" he asked.

I glared at him. "Tease," I muttered.

He really did move back to the television and put in a movie. He sat on the couch and patted the spot next to him, motioning for me to sit. I crossed my arms in irritation, but I did join him. He put his arm around me and tucked me into his side, turning his head long enough to kiss the top of my head.

"What just happened?" I finally asked. "Why'd you go all cold on me? And you're blocking your thoughts, so I can't tell?"

He cringed. "I'm sorry. It's just weird."

His words hurt like a sword stabbing me through the heart. I knew he felt my pain too when he leaned forward and turned to face me with concern written all over his face.

"Not you, Ember. It's just, it's just this is your parent's house," he tried to explain.

I shrugged. "So? It's my house too." It took me a second to understand what he was saying. He hadn't touched me or let me touch him at his house. Was this some weird kind of respect? "Chad, we already had sex in this house," I reminded him.

"But this time they're home, like right down stairs or down the hall," he started.

I laughed. "So what?"

"Ember," he said in a serious voice.

"Do you want me to ask them to leave?"

"What? No way. You'd never do that," he told me.

"Not to Dad, but Mom will understand." I picked up my phone to call her. I thought it was ridiculous, but my body was on fire. I'd been sleeping with Chad for days without being able to really touch him. The week had turned into this insurmountable game of foreplay and we were finally, truly alone and he goes cold because my parents are home?

Chad grabbed my phone. "Shit, you really would, wouldn't you?"

I laughed, then remembered my original plan. As he was holding the phone as far from me as possible, I faked a move to reach it that had me straddling his lap. I had a momentary hesitation that maybe he just really didn't want me, but that was quickly laid to rest as I physically felt his response to my new position. I rolled my hips against him as he sucked in a sharp breath and I fought back a moan.

I leaned down and kissed him. My phone hit the plush carpeted floor with barely a sound as it slipped from his hand. There was no hesitation as he kissed me back.

He broke only long enough to ask, "Shouldn't we at least lock the door?"

I pulled my shirt off and tossed it on the floor in response. He groaned, but his hands roamed up my body and quickly disposed of my bra. There was no more talk about my parents. I threw my head back in victory as his mouth sought out my breasts.

"So beautiful," he said as he began worshipping my body.

Normally this time of year, as I fought not to gain too much weight and inevitably did anyway, I was prone to bouts of depression. I noticed the extra pudge on my waist, but when he told me I was beautiful, I believed it. Not just that, but I felt the truth of it through our bond.

I stood up long enough to let Chad undo my pants and pull them down. I took the time to strip him of his clothes too before resuming my initial position. His hands blazed a path of fire across my already heated skin as his gentle but persistent touches had me shaking in waves of pleasure sooner than I'd expected. The smug look on his face told me he didn't mind one bit.

Like some weird orchestrated dance, we got up and moved to the bed, never breaking our connection as we continued to kiss across the room. I was ready to resume my position on top, but Chad had other things in mind as he gently laid me down but didn't join me on the bed.

I started to pout, then I saw flashes of pictures in his head seconds before he acted them out. That quick anticipation and seeing myself through his eyes while he feasted on my body was the most erotic thing I'd ever experienced. I didn't think anything could top it until he hovered over me and we joined as one—mind, body, and soul.

As we both began to climax, sharing our feelings and images openly with each other, my front teeth began to elongate. Chad pulled back to see them for himself then smiled to show me his too. He stared down at me trying to decide. I saw an image of his teeth sinking into my neck flash through my mind and I hesitated.

A brief sadness washed through our bond, but he nodded and leaned down to kiss my lips, ignoring the call to seal our bond as he continued to make love to me until my body began spasming uncontrollably and that feeling of letting go had me soaring. We didn't speak as he pulled back the covers and I scooted into bed, snuggling next to him

He hadn't said the words I love you yet, and neither had I. We hadn't even shared them through the bond, but I could feel it in the way he protected me, the way he touched me, and the way he cared. So why did I hesitate?

That one question burned inside me. What was I waiting for? I wasn't scared, or even nervous about a future with him. Sure, it seemed odd to be ready for such a commitment when we were still so young, but it was right for us.

I had told my parents that I was worried about the press and what people would say, but truthfully that had never bothered me before. I was mildly concerned about what it would mean to my mother's reputation, but she was among the top elite in her field and this really wouldn't hurt her career in any way.

I wasn't sure why I was hesitating when Chad was clearly ready for us to leap into the next stage. Everything was moving at such a fast pace. I think the human side of me was just rebelling against that.

"Don't worry about it," Chad said, stroking my hair and clearly listening to my thoughts.

"I hate disappointing you," I confessed.

"You're not. I swear," he said.

"I could feel your sadness, Chad."

"Em, it's okay. We have forever. I need you to want it as much as I do, and I know that will come in time. I'm not rushing you into anything."

"I know. You're amazing and understanding and I think that makes me feel a hundred times worse," I teased, but there was some sincerity to it too. "It's still early. We could watch that movie if you want," I offered.

"How about we stay right here. I prefer you naked and in my arms anyway."

I laughed. "No one said we had to get dressed to move to the couch."

"True, but I have a different idea. I think you'll like it," he said. I searched his mind but couldn't determine what he was up to. "Stay put. I'll be right back."

He walked over and first locked my bedroom door. His paranoia over my parents catching us was cute and comical. They were well aware he was staying over and wouldn't dare interrupt us. Given the circumstances, I wouldn't even get a lecture about it later.

After he was confident we wouldn't be disturbed, he turned off the lights. The room went pitch black as the sun had already set in the sky hours earlier. A light appeared, and then I saw he was using his cell phone to get around. He stopped at my bookcases and examined them thoroughly, finally choosing one, he turned and walked back to the bed. Climbing in I moved back into my usual position of him as my personal body pillow.

He positioned the phone on his chest, but I reached up and pulled my reading light over and turned it on instead.

"Perfect," he said. "Don't laugh. I haven't read aloud in quite some time, but these were always my favorite, probably always will be. Go ahead and tell me I'm a dork."

"You chose Harry Potter, and you picked it off of my bookshelf. That's the coolest thing ever. Do you know what house you're in?"

He chuckled and shook his head. *Hufflepuff,* he thought.

Me too. Maybe we really are true mates after all.

That's what I've been trying to tell you!

I laughed, calming immediately as he began to read. I was mesmerized by the soothing baritone of his voice. He was quite animated and changed it up for each new character. By the time Harry set foot into Hogwarts for the first time, I was fighting sleep, yet turned on more than ever. Could there possibly be anything sexier than my mate reading me my all-time favorite book? I wasn't sure there was.

Somewhere along the way I drifted off to sleep, lulled by the cadence of his voice.

Chad

Chapter 21

My body shook all over. It took me a minute to get my bearings straight.

"Chad, wake up," I heard a male voice say.

I groaned and stretched. Ember was still at my side. I wrapped my arms around her and snuggled back into the pillow.

"Chad, wake up," I heard again.

Slowly, I opened my eyes. Martin Kenston's face was hovering just over me. I jumped and tried not to squeal like a little girl. My heart was racing.

"Martin?" I asked sounding like I was still in a dream-like state.

"It's getting late. We need to get moving," he said.

"Um? Where exactly?" I asked trying to wake up.

"We tee off at seven. Come on," he insisted.

"Tee off?"

"Golf," Ember said with a moan. "Dad, Chad doesn't even play golf," she mumbled, sounding irritated we woke her.

"I thought I locked the door," I said aloud.

"You did. No need. I have keys to every room," Martin said.

"Oh," was all I can manage.

Shit! I'm naked, I thought.

Are you going? Ember asked.

I think I have to.

Probably for the best, she admitted.

"Are you two doing that mind thing again?" he asked, still sounding fascinated by our telepathy.

"Sorry sir," I apologized.

"Get out and let him get dressed," Ember told him.

I looked around the room awkwardly, anywhere that didn't require me to meet her father's eyes.

"Okay. Clothes are at the foot of the bed. I'll be in the kitchen grabbing a snack. We'll have breakfast at the club in a few hours," Martin said and then he turned and walked out of the room.

I groaned. "Golf? I don't know anything about golf. I've never even set foot in a Country Club before."

"Relax. He'll likely introduce you around to his friends. Shake hands, smile. There's nothing to it."

I pulled the covers back and got out of bed. The clothes he left were nothing like I would ever wear, not even for formal pictures that Mom required we dress up for. There was a pair of khaki pants, a navy and white oxford shirt, with a matching navy vest.

"This is what I have to wear to play golf?"

I dressed as directed and twirled around to show Ember. She giggled.

"You look very handsome, but definitely not you. It's best to think of it as acting. You're playing a character for the day. It's not so bad. You can even get away with stuff you normally wouldn't. At least that's how I get through public outings."

"I thought the Club was private."

"Oh it is, but trust me, you're on display the entire time you're there. I think Mom and I are meeting you guys for lunch. If you really don't want to go, I'll put a stop to him. It's up to you."

"No, it's okay. I'll go ahead and go. You put up with my family and their craziness. It's my turn to step out of my comfort zone. I can do this," I said, sounding more confident than I felt.

"It will definitely make him happy," she grumbled. "I'd rather have you naked and back in bed."

"Now that is a really tough offer to pass up." I flashed her a picture of what I'd rather be doing. She moaned, and I started to get hard. Time to get out of here.

It took me a few wrong turns, but I eventually found my way back to the kitchen. He tossed me a granola bar and handed me a glass of orange juice. I gulped it down quickly and soon we were off.

As we stepped outside, there was a driver waiting to take us. Martin handed him two sets of clubs that had been waiting by the front door. He clapped his hands together in excitement and waited for me to climb into the backseat before sliding in beside me.

I had never been chauffeured anywhere before. I couldn't afford a limo or anything for prom and had driven my date myself. This was already out of my comfort zone.

"So tell me, Chad. What do you like to do?" he asked.

Besides your daughter? was the first thought in my mind, but thankfully for once it didn't just pop out of my mouth. He had been gracious about not commenting when he found me naked in bed with Ember. I wasn't going to push my luck with a comment like that.

I cleared my throat. "Well, lots of things I guess. I love the outdoors."

"Great, well, perhaps you'll find a love for golf then. You've really never played before?"

"I'm afraid not, sir. Putt-putt with my siblings is probably about the closest thing I've ever done."

"So you're not an only child. How'd Ember handle that?" he asked, chuckling.

I smiled. "Better than I expected if I'm being honest. I'm the oldest of thirteen, so it was a bit of a shock to her."

"Thirteen children and you're the oldest? I'd say she was more than a little shocked. My poor little pumpkin. I hope it didn't overwhelm her too much. She looked good coming home last night. Normally a setting like that would have her locked up in her rooms for days with her nose stuck in a book," he confessed.

"It was much worse than that at Thanksgiving dinner. Mom always invites family and friends over to join us. There was probably close to fifty people. Ember did great. She even seemed to have a good time," I said proudly.

"You must be really good for her then. Even as a little girl she hated large parties. She is very much a loner. It's odd seeing how attached she's become to you. Mind if I ask how the two of you met?"

I smiled. "In the library."

He rolled his eyes and again I saw so much of Ember in him. "Why am I not surprised. Tell me she's not just spending her days wasting away in the library. Her mother and I were hoping she would open up and live a little while away at college."

I could hear how worried he was about my mate. It made me instantly like the man.

"She's not the biggest fan of parties, but I've dragged her to a few. She's fine when she gets there," I said.

He smiled. "She puts on a good front, son."

The endearment took me by surprise, but also made me feel like maybe I could be accepted as a part of his small family.

"She can't exactly hide things from me, remember?"

He shook his head and grinned. "That is just so amazing. I can't even imagine. I've heard of it, of course, but never seen it up close or had anyone to really ask about it, so forgive me if I get a little overzealous and try to pick your brain. Don't be afraid to tell me to back off. Ember sure won't."

I had noticed she was more open and candid with her parents than anyone else in her life. Truth be told, aside from a few friends she mostly kept at arm's length, Alicia and Martin were truly her entire world.

I glanced up at the driver before us. Martin saw my hesitation. I wasn't used to speaking so openly about my life, my family, and certainly not the unique bond with my mate.

Sensing my anxiety about it, he leaned forward and placed his hand flat against a glass barrier.

"You're safe to speak openly here, Chad. I would never endanger my daughter in any way. Her mother and I go to great lengths to keep what she is hidden. It's one of the reasons that despite the size of our house, we keep no staff. We had a small army at our disposal when Ember was little, everything from a cook to a guy whose sole responsibility was to clean up poop in the yard behind her dog." He chuckled. "The day she shifted for the first time took us all by surprise and changed our lives forever. The staff was all given severance and told they were no longer needed. The media got wind and suspected we'd lost our fortune. Eventually, those rumors died off, but we never rehired a permanent household staff. Sure, there's a housekeeper that comes in once a week to dust and deep clean, but otherwise Alicia and I handle everything ourselves."

"Why is that? I mean you can afford to hire staff, even top-notch staff with a gag order," I said.

"That is true, but a gag order is nothing more than a piece of paper, Chad. It doesn't guarantee anyone's loyalty. People talk, especially when someone like my wife is involved. That is our home. That is our daughter's home, and she needs to feel safe to live and thrive. I knew she had to have a safe place to shift and explore that new part of her."

The love he showed for his adopted daughter was astounding to me. He truly did love her unconditionally. Not just that but would do anything to protect her.

"You and Alicia are pretty amazing people. Most humans would have freaked out and tossed her out. You know that's true. There's a reason we keep to ourselves and don't reveal ourselves to your kind," I said. "Ember told me you somehow knew about shifters and helped her understand what was happening when she began to change. How? I don't understand how you could possibly have known, let alone be able to truly help her."

He took a deep breath and nodded. I noticed him twirling a ring on his right ring finger. It was unique. I had never seen anything like it before.

"Much in the way you aren't supposed to share your secrets, I harbor my own. Ancient secrets passed down from parent to child, generation after generation, since the dawning of time. I had planned to induct Ember and someday her husband when she came of age. For all intents and purposes that would be you now. But there's a dilemma here. Because the Order of the Verndari's biggest secret is you."

"Me?" I asked, not following.

"The Verndari protect shifters, Chad. We always have, and we always will. I won't pretend it's a perfect organization. Some of the younger people want to see things change, not necessarily expose you, but use you, I suppose. We've taken down a few small segments already. They are now calling themselves the Verndari Raglans. It's like a war is brewing within the Order. It's going to take strong young people like you and Ember to maintain our ways, but to put the two of you in that position," he stalled and shook his head. "I just don't know. If anyone found out what you are, Chad, I just don't know how they'd react."

I took a moment to let his words sink in. These Verndari, they were humans and they knew about shifters? I had never heard of such a thing, yet Ember had told me her father knew things no human should know. Now he was telling me there were more, possibly lots more just like him?

"Truth is, son, most of the Verndari have never actually met someone like you. There are those of us that work more hands on, but the rest just know in abstract, much like a fairytale. In fact, most of those stories you've heard were put out there by us, as a way to help hide shifters. I'm always fascinated by the old tales and the lengths my ancestors went to, in order to hide the truth from other humans."

Before I had a chance to press him for more information, the car came to a stop.

"Ah, we're here. Game face on, follow my lead. I'll make a golfer of you yet," he said completely changing his tone like he didn't just rock my entire world with his revelations.

We waited for the chauffeur to park and walk around to open the door. Martin exited the vehicle first, and I slid over to get out behind him. I felt awkward in the borrowed clothes. I knew my weight was starting to pack on and I was a little self-conscious in the outfit as it was a bit on the snug side.

I looked around while Martin retrieved the clubs, passing one set to me. I watched him sling his easily over one shoulder. I tried to duplicate, but the thing was bulkier than I had judged, and I nearly knocked myself over. I heard someone snicker nearby, but Martin either didn't notice or was kind enough not to draw attention to it.

We walked into the Club like he owned the place. Everyone we passed stopped and nodded a quick hello. We stopped by the front desk and he introduced me there and confirmed our tee time.

"Will others be joining us, sir?" I asked, hoping beyond hope that the answer was no.

"No, son, it's just the two of us this morning." Relief washed over me. "Alicia thought it would be best if we got to know each other without the distractions of others, and since you've never played the game before, it's probably for the best."

I cringed. I knew I was about to embarrass him regardless of whether others were with us, or just close enough to witness the impending disaster.

We didn't have to wait; we walked through the Club to the back of the building where a golf cart was waiting. Two caddies were also there, but Martin dismissed them saying their services were not needed.

I assumed he knew I'd embarrass even his caddies. I wasn't looking forward to this, but I knew he was important to Ember, and so I vowed to at least make an attempt.

Martin drove after we secured the clubs and I slid into the seat next to him. We didn't talk as we rode along to the first hole.

I said a quick prayer I wouldn't look like more of an idiot than I already felt and mimicked Martin's movements with a little more caution than I had while attempting to sling the bag over my shoulder.

He took a deep breath and stretched. "I just love the smell of fresh air on a new morning."

Now that I could appreciate. I loved the outdoors and looking around at the nearby trees lining the beautiful green grass. I began to relax. "Me too," I admitted.

He took out his first club. I knew enough to know they were all different, but I had no idea what to use, or which one should be used and when. I figured it would be best to just try and pretend I could at least pick out the right club to start with—even though they all looked pretty similar to me.

Martin stuck a peg in the ground then balanced the golf ball on top of it. He stood back up, lined up his hands on the club, pulled back and swung in a clean, crisp motion stopping the club in midair near his shoulder as the ball went soaring into the air.

"Your turn. Let's see what you've got," he said, turning to me.

I gulped, took a deep breath and tried my best to follow his lead. First, I grabbed the wrong club and he had to correct me. Then my peg thing, or "tee" as he informed me, wasn't seated in the ground correctly and my ball kept falling off. Finally, I was ready to take my swing. I faced off, standing exactly where and how he was. I lined up my club with the ball and pulled back, just as I'd seen him do, and I let that club swing.

I missed the ball entirely and nearly fell on my ass. Apparently, that club swings faster and more powerfully than I expected, and I didn't stop in midair like Martin had. Nope, I kept swinging and I nailed myself in the back, dropping it to the ground with a few chosen curse words flying from my mouth.

Martin stood there staring at me as a grin slowly creeped across his face and he folded over holding his stomach as he roared with laughter. Tears were streaming down his face until he finally stopped laughing, stood up gasping for air and trying to ask if I was okay.

"I'm fine," I said, feeling more embarrassed the longer he laughed.

"I'm sorry, it's just, if you could have seen yourself. It was like something out of a movie."

I broke down and laughed alongside him. "I told you I've never played before."

"I just didn't expect you to be quite that bad," he confessed.

I shook my head and grinned. "Is that why you sent the caddies away? Didn't want me embarrassing you in front of anyone?"

He sobered up quickly, though I had only been joking.

"No, not at all. The members of this Club are all Verndari, Chad. Those boys are next generation members trying to make a few extra bucks. I knew you had questions and I thought it best if we were alone to talk openly. I promise that's all that was."

"Oh. Well, thank you for telling me that. I do have so many questions."

"Please, ask," he said, and I hoped he didn't regret that invitation before I was done.

"Okay, how is this even possible? Humans don't know about my kind. We don't discuss it, most of us don't even associate with your people. It keeps us safe. We have to hide from the world because they wouldn't understand or accept us otherwise, but you're telling me that for many generations your people, these Verndari have known?"

"Chad, the Verndari have been around since the creation of shifters. Where your history stems from the people chosen to carry God's animals into the new world in the days of Noah. . ."

I interrupted him. "Wait, wait, wait. How could you possibly know that story? It's never been written down anywhere. It's passed verbally through stories to the children of every shifter."

"Exactly, as have the stories of the descendants of Noah, God's chosen family to protect his shifters in the next age: the Verndari."

I was speechless. I didn't know what to think or say to that. Was it possible? I mean it made sense, but wow, hearing him say it just blew my mind. How did I not know this?

"I've never heard of the Verndari, Martin. How can two secrets that great have stayed segregated all these years? I mean you clearly know about us. Why don't we know about you?'

"One of our prime directives is to protect shifters, without interfering. It's only been in the last decade that we've slowly begun to change that, and honestly, many are not happy about it. There's also a rogue group of young people on the rise looking to expose you, the Raglans. It's been a nightmare keeping them in check. Incidents of disappearing shifters are on the rise, and they move as quickly as we shut them down, using our own resources even."

"What do they want with us? I mean, they have to know we aren't going to harm anyone, especially my kind."

Martin laughed. "Chad, do you really think I'd let just anyone, true mate or not, near my daughter if I didn't know without a doubt you could protect her and care for her? I started asking around about you the second Ember mentioned your name. And do you know what I heard?"

"I think I'm afraid to ask, sir," I said. I didn't blame him for checking up on me, but it didn't make it any less unsettling to hear his admission.

"Chad is one badass squirrel and as protective of those he cares about as any wolf. I heard you single handedly took down a tiger and fought valiantly against the big cats last spring."

I laughed. "The Westins. You had mentioned you were friends with Patrick, but never got around to saying just how you know him."

Martin sighed. "I'm really not supposed to know him, and we weren't supposed to interfere. We weren't actually, only observing. It was Patrick who found us. When we see odd things happening or shifter movements that aren't normal, we go in for observation. So I was on a mission in upstate after word came in that a couple of Bulgarian wolves entered the country. These guys were known to cause trouble, so we came prepared."

"Prepared?"

"Tranquilizers." He grimaced. "We don't use them often, but our ultimate job is to protect your secrets, even if that means taking down those rare shifters that draw attention to you. Do you understand?"

"That makes sense," I said.

"So we tracked them to this house in a secluded area and they show up with a girl. They carried her in and she looked sick. In reality, she was heavily drugged."

"Elise," I said softly.

Martin nodded. "Patrick was tracking his mate. He was frantic and would have done anything to save her. We didn't even hear him stalk us from behind, but he stayed quiet and listened. When he was certain we weren't going to harm him or Elise, he broke his most sacred vow and showed himself to us."

"Wow, he must have been desperate for help to do that," I said.

Martin nodded. "He was. I have been watching and protecting shifters my entire life, but never in my wildest dreams would I ever have thought I would get to see one change up close like that. One minute he's this menacing wolf with intelligent eyes, and the next he's naked as the day he was born, standing before us. I'll never forget that moment."

"So what did you do?"

"Once we recovered from the shock, we worked together to cause a distraction and rescue her. We had to use the tranquilizers I'm afraid. They were terrible men, but I still find it inhumane for any reason, even when necessary. They were taken to one of our facilities designed to rehabilitate rogue shifters. Unfortunately, these facilities at some point began research on them. It disgusts me." He stopped speaking and looked around, making sure no one was nearby. "Chad, I work closely with the Westins and a very small elite group of Verndari that are trying to infiltrate these centers and weed out who's behind the movement. As a scientist, my skills are highly sought after for recruitment. I've been undercover to take down a few. It's a very fine line to walk. The science behind studying your DNA is fascinating, but the manner in which they are going about it is just wrong. I do only what I have to. It's the only way to ensure that we put an end to it all, permanently."

I was struggling to fully comprehend everything he was trying to say. But even more so why. "Why are you telling me this, Martin?"

"What are you majoring in, Chad?"

"Science, sir. I haven't confirmed my focus yet, probably genetics or bio-chemistry." As I said it, dawning set in. He's already admitted to investigating me, so of course he knew that already.

Martin smiled. "By marrying Ember, I can officially recruit you as Verndari. Actually, they would become more suspicious if I didn't. Do you understand?"

"That makes sense, but they could never know about me," I said adamantly. After everything he'd just told me, working for these people scared the shit out of me.

"Damn right," Martin confirmed. "We've gone to great lengths to keep Ember's identity a secret. Everyone here believes her records were falsified to allow her to go undercover. But there are Verndari inside your school."

"What? Does she know this?"

"No, she doesn't, but that's the lengths I've gone to protect her. It's the perfect cover story. She's a writer, an observer. That's the role they believe she's playing there."

"Martin, you have to tell her!" I said a little too loudly. Quickly I lowered my voice and looked around. No one was in sight.

"She doesn't need to know," he insisted.

"Listen to me, if these Verndari are watching her, then yes she needs to know. If you really know anything about my kind, then you already know the signs to watch for in mating pairs. We haven't taken any precautions to hide that, and I'm registered as a squirrel shifter with the school. They would already know who I am."

We had continued to play through while we talked, though I hadn't bothered to take another whack at the ball and he hadn't suggested it. He stopped as he bent over to place his ball on the tee at the fifth hole, straightening and turning to look me in the eyes.

"I told you I have gone to great lengths to protect my daughter's true identity. Do you think for one second I haven't already thought through this? Cormack Shannahan is the only one at the ARC who knows who you really are, but the few others there are all within my trusted circle. I would not leave a threat like that close to Ember. With Cormack's help and that of Patrick's team, we've doctored your files to make it appear that you and your family are from a low level Verndari clan. This comes with certain benefits, including that new job your father will be offered next week."

"What?" I asked. My mind was whirling with mobster stories, because that's exactly what it sounded like to me. How had I gotten mixed up in any of this?

"You have nothing to fear. Your father applied for the job himself, but because we had previously made it appear that you too, are a young undercover Verndari agent at Archibald Reynolds College, he was flagged in our database as soon as he applied for the job. Don't worry, we listed your family as extremely low-level, with you as the first true recruitment from there because of your relationship with Ember. No one will dive any deeper than that, and his title will not even warrant him a crescent ring. That way no one from the organization would ever reach out to him in any way."

"Still, we have to warn him, just in case," I insisted.

Martin thought it over and nodded. "Perhaps that would be the prudent thing given the circumstances."

"He's not even supposed to find out if he's in the running for it until next week. He was telling me about it while I was home."

"That's good then. Perhaps we can intercede in time. Since he's flagged as Verndari, he'll receive top pay from the company. It could benefit your family greatly, but on the offhand that someone does approach him, bringing him into the loop may be necessary. Tell me, Chad, can we trust him with this?" Martin asked me seriously.

"Oh, he's going to freak out at first, but yes, we can trust him."

"Honestly, having him working at one of our holding companies will only make your back story all the stronger. And when you graduate, you'll have to decide whether you wish to begin your career or continue on with higher education. The Verndari take care of their own. By the time you return to school on Monday, you'll find your school loans have been paid off in full. Obviously, if you wish to continue on for your master's that too will be covered."

"What? That's insane. It's too much. I can't accept that," Chad said.

"Chad, the Verndari are a very old, very rich, and very established organization. Now that you're in the system, you're one of us, and I told you we take care of our own. You and Ember will never have to worry about finances. You can choose where you wish to live anywhere in the world as well as what you want to do. Higher education? Medical school? Teaching? Pharmaceuticals? Perhaps you'd even consider staying local and working alongside me in research and development. There are so many doors about to open to you, son."

I didn't know what to think or say. "It's a lot to take in, Martin. Can I think it over and let you know? I probably should discuss all of this with Ember too," I added.

Martin grinned and slapped me on the back. "Absolutely."

He stepped up to his tee and pulled back to swing.

"Enough business talk for now, Chad. I think it's time you really learned to play golf."

I laughed. "I think we both know that's a terrible idea."

"Nonsense, come here," he said. He guided me towards the tee, physically positioning me where he wanted me to stand, then he kicked at my feet until they were spread exactly as he wished. "Very good. Here, take mine," he offered, handing me his club. "Now," he said standing directly behind me. I started to move when his arms wrapped around me. "No, don't move. Just like this," he said as he held his hands over the tops of mine, pressed up against my back, and physically moved my arms to demonstrate.

To say I was uncomfortable would be putting it mildly.

Ember

Chapter 22

Mom and I arrived at the club a little early. We had stopped at one of our favorite little boutiques on the way to do some shopping. To my joy, it had been pretty uneventful, which also meant no holdups. Knowing it was a regular occurrence, we always left extra time on our outings. You never knew when a fan would approach, or paparazzi would show up and stall our day. It was usually a given, but this time the morning passed quickly and quietly.

Deciding on massages at the Club where we were meeting Dad and Chad for lunch, we arrived earlier than planned.

Just as I was settled down onto the table and Heidi began to rub out the tension in my neck and shoulders, I got the weirdest feeling. I wasn't sure what it was, but my muscles tensed as I thought of Chad.

"Oh, Emmy, I'm glad you came to see me today. You are so tense. Deep breaths, and try to relax," Heidi said in a soothing voice.

Chad, is everything okay? You're sending weird vibes through the bond, I said.

No. Everything is not okay. We're in the middle of a field and your father is basically spooning me!

I started to giggle. I tried to hold it back, but it exploded from me in a full belly laugh. I assumed Dad was trying to teach him basic form, but the description he gave made me cry from laughing so hard.

"Ma'am? Are you okay? Emmy? Should I fetch your mother?" Heidi asked, concerned by my outburst.

"No, no. I'm fine. Sorry, Heidi," I said as tears continued to flow down my cheeks, and I fought to hold back more laughter.

Great, my masseuse thinks I'm going insane. Thanks for that, I teased.

Glad you got a good laugh. I don't think I'll ever really learn this game. Especially now that I've been traumatized for life.

I could feel that he was over his initial freak out and just being silly now. The image of my father holding him from behind in the same way he had done when I was a little girl and learning the game was just too hysterical.

Tell you what. There's a golf course at the ARC. How about I teach you when we get back?

Hmmm, replace your Dad with you and I may learn to love this game.

When my time with Heidi was up, I felt rejuvenated and more relaxed than I had felt in a long time. My stomach rumbled. I was starving.

What hole are you up to? I asked Chad as I left the room. Mom was waiting just outside the door.

"I wonder where your father and Chad are? I hope they don't take too much longer. I'm hungry," she said.

We're only on the seventh hole. How many are there anyway?

Really? Are you going for the longest game in history? I teased. *Tell Daddy to play through and stop at the ninth for lunch.*

The ninth hole conveniently ended back at the Clubhouse, just outside the main restaurant. It was a common stopping point for business, or those who didn't have time to play through all eighteen holes.

"They're on the seventh hole. I told him to tell Daddy to play through and meet us for lunch," I told her.

She looked confused for a moment because I didn't even have my phone in my hand. I needed to remember to use that as a prop more often. I slyly pointed to my head.

"Oh," she said, a little surprised. "From that far?" she asked, lowering her voice to a whisper.

I shrugged. "Distance doesn't seem to be an issue."

"That's so weird, isn't it? Always having him there like that?"

"I don't know, you sort of get used to it after a while. I don't really know how to explain it. At first I just wanted him gone, but now if he stays quiet for too long it makes me worry."

"Tell me you're happy. Really happy, Ember," Mom said.

"I know, it's crazy, but I really am. I mean, we're still getting to know each other, but he's such a great guy, Mom."

"Not too hard on the eyes either," she commented with a grin giving me a quick hug.

"Definitely not," I agreed.

"Let's go ahead and grab a table. We can get some drinks and maybe an appetizer while we wait."

"Great idea," I said. "I'm starving."

My parents belonged to a few Country Clubs in the area. This was my dad's favorite. I had fond memories of growing up here with the other children. Everyone was down to Earth and real, not like the celebrity places we frequented with my mom. There were rarely any celebrities here. I hadn't noticed or given it much thought growing up. It was kind of nice to just be normal here.

When I shifted for the first time and Dad started telling me about the Verndari, I realized that this Club was all Verndari. Everyone wore the same ring or pendant. It was apparent they were as influential as some of Mom's most exclusive events or places. It also made me nervous just being there. They didn't know who I was, and they never could. It had once been a sanctuary away from the spotlight for me, and now I dreaded coming here.

Mom and I were given a table by the big picture window overlooking the golf course. We ordered drinks and mozzarella sticks to tide us over while we waited. The waiter returned several times, asking if we were ready to order, but Mom dismissed him each time.

Walking in now, Chad warned me about a half hour later just as they entered the dining room.

The sight of the two of them together made my heart flutter. Chad looked as though he fit in better than I did. It took me a minute to fully accept that this was going to be our life. He was a part of it, a part of my family now.

As they reached the table, Chad leaned down and kissed my cheek affectionately in the same manner my father was greeting my mother. From the strange look on his face when he took notice, I didn't think it had been planned.

Once we were all seated, the waiter ran back over quickly. We ordered our meals and he left us.

"So, what took you so long? That was a long eight holes," Mom teased.

Dad cut comical eyes towards Chad.

"Hey, don't blame me, sir. I told you it was a bad idea," Chad defended.

Images of Chad's ball stuck in a sand pit as he tried feverishly to hit it back out floated through my mind. I bit my bottom lip so not to give it away, though when the vision shifted to show my dad falling, as he somersaulted down the embankment landing hard in the sand below. Chad's attempt at helping him had me biting back a laugh.

I shot him a look to cut it out and he grinned before shutting out the memory.

Mom stared back and forth between the two of us. "I don't want to know, do I?"

"No, you really don't," I said still fighting back laughter.

The food arrived and we all chatted and enjoyed a nice meal together. Before we got up to leave, there was a squeal from across the room. I turned just in time to see a pink blur come flying at me. Arms wrapped around me tightly.

"Emmy! You hardly ever come to the Club anymore and I've missed you so much." I knew from the voice and the death grip around my neck that Mia Rose was in town. She pulled back to look at me. "Love the glasses. How's school? Oh," she lowered her voice conspiratorially, "I heard you were undercover at one of those shifter colleges. How is that going?"

I shot Dad a look, and he smiled and slightly nodded his encouragement. I had been wondering what he was telling his Verndari friends. I supposed this explained a lot, but how was I supposed to explain Chad?

Your dad has already covered that too. Apparently I'm also undercover, since I just transferred last spring, mid-year it was an easy sell. Though how, when everyone there knows who and what I am, is beyond me, but that's our cover story, Chad told me.

"I can't even believe it. Getting an assignment so young and working so close to them. How cool is that? I'm so jealous."

I scoffed. "Mia Rose, you're at Harvard," I reminded her.

She brushed it off. "I know, but seriously, nothing but a bunch of stuck up assholes there," she said before turning towards my parents. "Sorry Mr. and Mrs. Kenston," she said sweetly, then turned back to me. "But it's true. The guys are horrible entitled pigs."

I had to laugh because I knew no one more entitled than Mia Rose. Mia and I had been the best of friends right up until my first shift. I had always been on the loner side, but I'd pulled away from everyone afterwards. A part of me missed her, but mostly I knew our friendship wasn't exactly deep. She'd spread rumors that I was on drugs and needed rehab as an explanation for my sudden retreat. I hadn't bothered to correct her. Better that than the truth.

"I'm sure we have a few pigs at my school too," I said, laughing at my own joke. Chad, Mom, and Dad all laughed along too, but Mia Rose seemed confused. "Pigs, cause they're shifters, get it?"

"Oh," she semi-laughed. "Pigs, funny. But seriously, are they cute at least?"

Mia was always the same, very self-absorbed and entirely shallow.

I shrugged. "Sure, some of them are. Oh, um, Mia Rose, this is Chad, my. . ." I hesitated.

"Boyfriend," Chad completed for me. "Hi, it's nice to meet you," he said rising to stand behind me and offering Mia his hand. She shook it while eyeing him openly.

A rage of jealousy shot through me as she looked him over like a piece of eye-candy. Chad grinned, feeling my discomfort and possessively wrapped an arm around my waist. His touch helped calm me.

"Boyfriend? Too bad, you are hot."

"Mia Rose," my mother said in that warning voice only mothers seemed to have.

"Sorry Mrs. Kenston, but I'm certain he already knows that. Lucky you, Emmy." She leaned in to whisper in my ear. "When you're done with him, I'm totally calling dibs on that."

I bit back the urge to claw her eyes out and smiled sweetly. "I wouldn't hold my breath if I were you. I have no intention of giving this one up."

"Oh, it's serious then?"

I could tell she was fishing for gossip and nothing more, so I didn't bother with a response.

Dad looked at his watch and sighed. "I'm afraid we might not finish our round today, Chad. I promised Alicia we'd escort our girls shopping this afternoon. Perhaps we'll pick up where we left off over Christmas break."

I shot Dad a thank you look. "Oh, sorry Mia Rose, but we really must be going. It was nice to see you again. Tell your parents hello," I said cordially.

You really hate her, don't you?

No, I insisted. *I just really hate the way she is drooling over you.*

As we turned to leave, I saw the smirk on Chad's face from my admission.

I was happy to see we made it back to the car with no further interruptions. As we were waiting out front for the valet to bring Mom's car around, Chad wrapped his arm around me. I leaned into his warmth like it was the most natural thing in the world.

My thoughts drifted off to what it would be like to truly be mated to him. How would things change? What would it mean for us? Would it hurt? The stories he'd told me equally intrigued me and grossed me out. I feared the unknown, making me nervous to take that leap. There was so much finality in it, or at least that's how it felt. It was the biggest forever decision I'd ever have to make, and yet it didn't feel like a decision at all, just the inevitable next step.

I could feel Chad's presence in my head, but he didn't say anything or acknowledge my thoughts. I liked that he left me alone to sort through my feelings.

The car arrived, and Chad and I slid into the back seat as Mom took the passenger seat, leaving Dad to drive.

"Your clubs, Martin," Chad reminded him.

"Already in the trunk, sir," the valet said, flashing a smile. He leaned down a little further. "Good to see you, Emmy."

"You to, Frederick," I said amicably. He wasn't one of my favorite people and he knew it. I was sure Dad tipped him much too well just for acknowledging me. We had grown up together, just a couple of Verndari kids thrown together at various events. A lot of us worked at the Club as teens and college aged adults. It was a good way to get to know people and get in stronger with the group. I was thankful my parents had never forced the issue and made me work there.

As we pulled out dad said, "Chad and I wanted to take his father out this afternoon. Guy stuff. What do you think of some shopping for just you ladies?"

Mom laughed. "After all these years putting up with our girl time, I think you've definitely earned some guy time." She leaned over and kissed his cheek. I smiled watching them. I couldn't remember a time they weren't loving with each other like that.

"Hey, if we're going by Chad's house to pick up his dad, can Carolyn come shopping with us?" I asked.

"That's his sister, right?" Mom asked.

"Yes, she's the one I told you about that loves high fashion and wants to be a designer."

"Well, let's see what kind of eye she has then. Think she can keep up with me?" There was a twinkle in Mom's eye as she teased.

"If anyone can, it'll be Carolyn," I said.

"You're serious?" Chad asked.

"Yeah. I mean, we need to clear it with her first. She may have plans already," I pointed out.

"She'll drop everything for this," he assured us.

"Good, well, let's call her and confirm it then," Mom suggested.

Chad looked at me one last time for confirmation before pulling out his phone. I could hear Carolyn readily and excitedly agreeing.

An hour later we pulled into their driveway. The younger kids were all outside playing in the yard and ran to the front to say hi to us. Mom's eyes misted over a little at the sight. I knew she had always dreamed of a big family with lots of children, but she hadn't been able to conceive, and the demands of her career hadn't made it feasible to adopt more kids. I constantly reminded her growing up that she had hit the jackpot of perfect kids and didn't need any more than me.

Chad's parents greeted us at the door. His mother hugged me as if I were already one of her own. She was rushing out the door with little Caitlyn in tow. Apparently, she wasn't feeling well and had an appointment to get to with a local shifter doctor, but not before I introduced them to my mom and dad. Introducing our parents to each other should have felt strange and premature, but it didn't.

Christian walked into the room with Carolyn a few minutes later.

"Returning him already?" he teased.

"Never," I assured him.

Carolyn squealed as she hugged me, and Cassie and Cammie begged to tag along. I said yes at the same time Carolyn said no.

Are we all going together? I asked Chad silently.

No, your dad and I are staying here. Is that a problem?

No, not at all, just checking.

"We have room. Let them come. They'll keep me company while you and Mom shop." I said, rolling my eyes. "By the way, Carolyn, this is my mother, Alicia. Mom, this is Carolyn I was telling you about, and this is Cammie and Cassie. They want to tag along too," I said.

"Oh great, you two will keep Ember from sheer boredom. She always whines and says I shop too much. But you, I understand you're ready to keep up and help me with a new wardrobe." She winked at Carolyn, who didn't squeal, or faint, though she did look like she wanted to. She simply nodded in shocked awe. That was the effect my mother had on people.

I gave Chad a quick kiss goodbye as Cole made a noise of disgust, then shooed the girls out. The three of them settled into the backseat. I assumed I was driving, but to my surprise Mom took the driver's seat.

"Um, Mom? You sure you don't want me to drive?" I asked.

"Just get in the car, Ember," she said, so I walked around and got into the passenger seat. She started the engine and backed out. "We aren't that far from Rodeo Drive, how about we start there?"

I rolled my eyes and stared out of the window. I knew what a mob scene that place could cause, but suspected she picked it for that very reason—give the girls a taste of stardom. I'd had enough of it for a lifetime personally. At least I was dressed appropriately since we'd just come from the Club.

As we pulled onto the highway, I glanced back and said a quick prayer. "Please make sure your seatbelts are on," I begged them.

"Ember!" Mom scolded.

"What? You're a terrible driver. I'm only looking out for their safety," I argued, then turned towards the back again. "Seriously, Mom is great at a lot of things, just driving and cooking aren't among those things."

Mom laughed. "It's true. I can't even cook toast without burning it!"

Our bantering seemed to relax Carolyn's nerves. She even started talking and asking questions, and by the time we arrived at the outlet she and Mom were well on their way to being fast friends, like some weird kindred spirits.

"Just valet park, please," I said.

She snorted. "Did you really think I'd do anything else?"

She pulled up in front of her favorite store and jumped out, tossing the keys to the nearest valet, not even bothering to wait for the ticket. I told Carolyn to keep up and she ran after her. I obtained our ticket, and the twins and I walked in. There was already a whirlwind of excitement surrounding Mom and Carolyn, but Carolyn was the one taking control of the situation and commanding everyone with what she wanted. I bit back a grin. The girl was born for this world.

Cassie and Cammie got into the hype for a little while, then grew bored with it. Slumping down into the chair next to me,

Cammie whined. "I never thought I'd say this, but I'm done shopping."

They each had several bags stuffed full of clothes, and I'd been right; Carolyn had an amazing eye for fashion, and mixed and matched Mom to perfection. They were both elated hours later.

"That was the most fun I've had shopping in ages!" Mom exclaimed. The valet could barely shut the trunk it was packed so full. "Carolyn, dear, perhaps we can do this again soon. Christmas will be here before we know it."

"It's my favorite time of year," Carolyn gushed.

The two of them chatted the whole drive back as I closed my eyes and started to drift off. I didn't open them again until we were back to the house. Mom and Carolyn were making plans for all of us to get together over my Christmas break.

Dad and Chad weren't there; they had apparently left with Manny to go out for dinner.

Are we waiting for you to get back? I asked Chad secretly.

No, your dad and I will drive Damon's car back so it's there for tomorrow.

Tomorrow?

Yeah, I have to pick them up at the airport at two tomorrow and head back to campus.

I pouted. *Were you planning to just leave me?*

Not if you'll come with me, he said, and I could feel the smile behind his words.

I started giving hugs and saying goodbye to everyone. Mom looked a little confused as I shooed her out of the door towards the car. I confiscated the keys from her and jumped into the driver's seat.

"What about your father?" she asked as she got in.

"They have a ride back. I didn't want to wait around."

Chad

Chapter 23

Dad and Martin seemed to hit it off quickly, but I knew there were far too many ears around for us to really talk. I suggested going out to dinner as an excuse to get us out of the house. I couldn't think of one single restaurant we could openly discuss all that needed to be said either. In the end, I settled on sandwiches and drove the three of us to the beach. It was off season and the section I'd chosen had very few people. Those that may be there would give us our space and the noise of the waves crashing over the shore would give us the privacy necessary, even if someone did come by too close.

I had grabbed a blanket from the house before leaving, and spread it down on the ground. Both men looked at me in confusion.

"We're having a picnic?" Dad finally asked. "On the beach? Isn't this something you should be sharing with Ember? This place looks deserted."

Martin's face lit up with understanding and he clapped his hand on my shoulder. "Brilliant idea. I would never have thought of it," he said.

I shrugged. "It's the first place I could think of where we could truly talk."

Dad still looked confused and hesitated as Martin dropped down onto the blanket. Slowly, he caved when the food came out and joined him. I sat down last, taking my sub Martin held out to me. We started eating in an awkward silence.

"Dad, have you ever heard of a group called the Verndari?" I blurted out.

He froze in mid bite, took his time chewing and finally nodded. "Sure I have. They're like our version of the boogieman."

I scrunched up my face in surprise by his answer. "Have you ever met one?"

"Chad, where's this coming from?" he finally asked. "I get Martin knows about Ember, but this isn't something I'm comfortable talking openly about. No offense," he said to Ember's dad.

"None taken," Martin returned.

After a few more awkward moments everything started bubbling out of me. I told my father about the Verndari, about Martin, and everything he'd already done and planned to do in the future. Then I told him about the job offer he would be receiving.

Dad smiled, seeming to take it all in far better than I ever dreamed.

"You really managed to get my family flagged as legitimate Verndari?" he asked Martin who only nodded still trying to puzzle out my dad's response. "You must have some hell of a high-level pull to make that happen." He sighed. "Already a done deal?"

"I'm afraid so. I needed to legitimize Ember's relationship to your son," Martin started.

"To protect your baby girl?"

"Yes."

"There's nothing I wouldn't do for my kids either, including taking a job with the enemy," he said. "I've seen what you people do to our kind. I actually appreciate what you've done already. Makes my job a hell of a lot easier."

"What?" I asked. "What job?"

"Chad, whatever he's told you about the Verndari, don't believe it. Don't let them suck you in the way they did me. Now, I stumbled into it by accident, and thank God they never dug deep enough or suspected what I was because that would have been very, very bad, but once you're in with these people, it's a life sentence. Don't let him fool you to believe they're the good guys. They aren't. The things I had to do to put food on our table and a roof over our heads would make you shudder. I'm not proud of it, but I did what I had to do at the time."

"What are you saying, Dad?"

"Chad, I already work for the Verndari. That job was already guaranteed to me, and part of the reason we moved the entire family out here. There are smaller factions within the organization. The one in particular I work for is an experimental group often on the outs with the overall faction. They are nuts, I mean certifiable nuts with a god complex. They snatch shifters off the streets and experiment on us, looking for ways to benefit humanity."

"The Raglans. You're part of the Verndari Raglans?" Martin said.

"I'm afraid so, and judging by the look on your face, I'm guessing you are not."

"No, but I work with an elite group of Verndari and shifters trying to track them down and put an end to those rogues. They are acting against everything we hold sacred. The Verndari were established to protect shifters, not hurt them. We have a strictly hands-off policy, observation only, unless it's something or someone that threatens the safety and secrecy of shifter-kind. My ancestors have gone to great lengths to ensure your protection. The Raglans threaten everything we believe. They're just a bunch of rogue spoiled brats who don't understand the consequences of their actions."

Dad stared at him with open curiosity. "Only one other man in the entire organization as long as I've known them has ever spoken that way. He said I was different than the others they'd recruited, and told me he was undercover and trying to shut down that faction. The only reason I'm still working for them is because of him. He was my one hope that these monsters would finally get what's due them. Heck, he even pulled some strings and a cover story about Chad to get him into the ARC mid-semester. Things were getting bad, and I had to get my family out of there before we were discovered."

"What?" I asked, shocked at everything Dad was confessing. "What's his name?"

Dad hesitated. "Look, I'll give up any other person in that organization before I'd rat him out."

"Dave? Is that your friend's name?"

Dad's eyes went wide and without verbally confirming it, Martin grinned and nodded. "You're gonna make me a believer in God at this rate, Chad. Dave is part of my team, Manny. We have only two somewhat on the inside. They started becoming too suspicious of John and he had to be pulled back for his own safety, of course, but Dave has managed to stay undercover. What I need to know is whether I can trust you to do the same," he said.

I gulped. What would happen if my dad didn't go along with the plan? What would Martin do to ensure his silence now that all this had come forth?

"I always hated those bastards. If you've got a plan to take them down, you can be damn certain I want in on it."

The two men shook hands and a new alliance was formed. I sat there and listened, my head in a fog trying to comprehend it all. It was decided that Dad would continue working for the Raglans, now undercover as a double agent. It was so James Bond, I felt like we were really living out a movie.

Ember and I would continue on throughout school, keeping a low profile, but there was no need for us to be secretive about what we are. The few Verndari within the ARC were already in the know, and from the outside all parties assumed we were just two undercover Verndari kids monitoring shifters up close. Naturally we would migrate to each other for support. In some weird way, it was a win-win situation for us all. I worried about Dad's role. He definitely had the biggest stake in this game, but he seemed happier, like some stress had been lifted from his shoulders.

Once he'd explained some of the things the Raglan's were doing, it all made sense and I understood why he was quick to jump on board and double cross them. They really were like the shifter boogieman stealing people right off the streets and holding them in cages to run experiments. He said they had nearly perfected a serum to keep shifters from shifting. That was the point where he'd freaked and tried to get out, but Dave had interceded with a proposition in California before he could, and Dad had jumped at the opportunity to get his family out of Vermont where apparently one of the main strongholds for the Raglans was currently.

I warned Martin I couldn't keep all of that from his daughter, not without detrimental harm to our bond.

Too late anyway. You've had an open line for most everything. Are you guys crazy? This is too dangerous. Your father can't put himself at risk like that.

He has to, Ember.

I know, but I don't have to like it.

Don't worry. We're all in this to keep my mom and sibling's safe. Don't give it another thought. This is a pretty plush job they're setting him up with. Minimal risk.

"She already knows, doesn't she?" Martin asked.

I nodded solemnly. "She's not happy about it, but she's really just worried for everyone. She'll be fine," I assured him.

Dad and Martin set up a weekly lunch date to keep in touch before we packed up and headed back to the car for a silent drive home. Each of us seemed lost in our own thoughts. I replayed events in my childhood that aligned with the stories Dad had shared. I knew the time we had spent living in that old oak tree outside the apartment Mom and the younger kids were crammed into was when he had tried to leave the Raglan's. They'd taken everything in a show of power.

I should have asked more questions. I should have seen he was in trouble. How much did Mom know? I still had so many unanswered questions. The cross-country move had weighed heavily on me. He had said he had a job lined up, and he did, but it hadn't lasted long. I knew now, it was only a waiting period till this new job became available. I had always wondered where he'd gotten the money for the new house. Why hadn't I asked more questions? Would he even have told me?

He did what he felt he had to do, Chad. You can't put all that on yourself.

I know, I said sadly.

We dropped Dad off at the house. I didn't bother to even go inside. I knew Mom would ask questions. She'd always been able to read me like an open book, and I was still processing too much for her not to sense something was off.

I hugged Dad.

"I love you, son," he said.

"Love you too, Dad."

In the end it really was just that simple. He loved his family and would do anything for us. I had always known it, but now I had a true glimpse into just what that meant to him.

Martin and I got into Damon's car, and I drove us back to the Kenston's house. I was grateful he had remained quiet, likely sensing my need for it. As I pulled into his driveway, he stopped me before getting out.

"Are we okay, Chad?" he asked.

"It's a lot to take in, but yeah, we're good. I'll stay the course. Ember will be safe with me at college. I'll reach out to the professors you noted and speak with Dean Shannahan. Just do me a favor and keep an eye out for my Dad. I don't like that he's already been involved in this all along," I said.

He nodded.

"How do you even know we can trust him?" I asked, feeling guilty for that very thought.

"Because he has more at stake than any of us. I'll call Dave and touch base just in case, but I think knowing what we're trying to do was a great relief to him. I don't put my trust in people easily, but our cards are played now. What's done is done. It's a wait and see now. See, it's never easy to face the unknown, but sometimes we have to take those leaps to move forward, son. This is one of those times. Fingers crossed it works out in our favor."

Ember

Chapter 24

I had caught enough of what was going on with Chad and the dads to understand the sticky situation we all found ourselves in. Chad was quiet when he got home, and we'd retreated to my room quickly.

He didn't want to talk about it, which worried me, but he didn't shut down our bond either, so I had a front row seat to all his concerns and questions plaguing him. I just held him and let him work through all his thoughts. Exhausted from a day out with Mom, Carolyn and the twins, I drifted off to sleep.

The next morning, Chad was back to his usual self. "Thanks for not pushing me to talk last night. I know it was a lot to take in. Are you okay?"

"Yeah, sure. I mean, I've always suspected my dad was involved in something like that."

"You know he's one of the good guys, right?"

I grinned. "Of course he is, and so is your dad."

"God, I hope so," he said still fighting uncertainty.

Mom had to return to work even though it was a Saturday. I asked Chad if he wanted to go on set with her and see the studio, but he declined. Secretly, I loved that he did. It was just another confirmation that he wasn't after Emmy Kenston, but just me, Ember.

Our time at home passed quickly. We went out for an early lunch with Dad, and all too soon we were saying goodbye and heading for the airport. I followed Chad over in my car. I hadn't had time to change into my college clothes, but since Magenta would be home for the holidays still, I wasn't all that concerned about it.

When Damon and Karis walked out of the terminal I got out of my car and met them on the curb. Karis squealed in delight as she ran over and hugged me.

"You're here! Chad was so worried you'd decided to turn tail and run that he was a complete mess when he dropped us off."

"Took your advice, Karis, and surprised her," he said grinning.

I hugged Damon next. "Glad you made the cut. I take it you're sticking around for good?"

I grinned and looked over at Chad. "I guess you're all stuck with me now," I confessed.

"Wait, did you?"

I cut Karis off before she could finish her thought. "Not yet, but we're getting there," I assured her.

She hugged me again. I was beaming when I pulled away to stand next to Chad. Another loud squeal rang out and I turned just in time to see two teenage girls running towards me.

"Oh my gosh! Oh my gosh! Oh my gosh! It's really you!" one of them said excitedly.

"I told you," the other insisted. "I told you she was Emmy Kenston. Can we get a picture with you?"

I immediately went into Hollywood mode. The smile planted on my face was fake and I assured them it was fine as I posed for a few shots.

"Is your mom here?" the first girl asked.

"No, I'm afraid not. I'm just picking up some friends before heading back to college."

They both looked a little disappointed. This was how things always went down.

"Could you tell her we asked about her? I'm Mandy, this is Jennifer."

"Mandy and Jennifer, it was really nice to meet you both. I'll be sure to tell Mom you said hello when I talk to her tonight."

"Come along girls, Emmy has things to do," the woman with them said. "Sorry, but thanks," she mouthed to me over their heads.

"Anytime," I politely mouthed back.

Karis and Damon were both staring at me like I had two heads. I sighed.

"What the hell was that all about? Emmy? Cute," he commented.

I rolled my eyes. "Can we just go before that turns into a full scene?" I asked starting to get nervous as I looked around.

"And what's with the fancy clothes you guys?" Karis asked.

Chad opened the passenger door to my car and I quickly hid inside, noticing a few people who had seen the girls' enthusiasm.

"Ember's mom is like famous, okay? Therefore, by association, I guess she is too. People stop them on the street all the time. It's very nerve-wracking going out in public. Little innocent things like that can turn into a big mob scene quickly."

I knew he was referring to his sisters' account of a small mob that attacked us on Rodeo Drive. Of course, that was expected, and Mom had been counting on it for their excitement, though it may have traumatized Cammie a little more than intended and we had to get security to break it up. Carolyn had called while we were out to lunch with my dad to thank me again and ended up telling her side of the story to Chad. It may have been a little over-exaggerated but had painted a clear picture for him.

"Seriously? Who's your Mom?" Karis asked.

"Alicia Kenston," I confessed.

"Wait, THE Alicia Kenston?" Damon asked.

"Yup," Chad and I said in unison.

"Like from. . ."

"Yup," I said cutting him off.

"And. . ."

"Yes, yes, and yes, THAT Alicia Kenston, the one and only."

"That's pretty cool. Why did we not know that?" Karis asked.

"It's not something I just tell everyone," I said.

"Why not?" Damon asked.

Karis shook her head at him. "I get it. You just want college to be about you," she said.

"Yeah. Maybe that's selfish, but that's exactly what I want."

"I understand. I'm not like some super Hollywood celebrity or anything, but I am heir to the Begay wolves in Alaska. Which means I'll be Pack Mother someday and Damon will be Alpha of our Pack. Growing up was hard because I could never decipher who my real friends were and who just wanted to get close to me to better their pack position. Coming to the ARC was pretty profound for me. It was the first time in my life I got to just be me, so I get it, you know?"

I felt like maybe Karis really did understand it. I nodded. "I know."

She leaned down and hugged me. "That's still pretty cool though and I'm totally telling Jenna. She's a huge fan of your mother's. Can I tell her I met her?"

I laughed. "Better than that. I think I'm going to have her visit soon. You can all meet her. She's been wanting to, but I made her promise to stay away. An Alicia-free zone, but she's my mom and I know that hurt her feelings. There's nothing that woman needs for Christmas, but I know that would mean the world to her."

Chad smiled down at me. "I think that's a great idea, and you're right, she'll love that."

"Okay, I think that group over there is convincing themselves to come over, so time to go. We can talk about all this at home," I said. The three of them all turned to stare down the group in question who backed down quickly and changed their course. I laughed. "Hey, you guys are even better than bodyguards."

We did say goodbye then. Damon and Karis got into their car and Chad jumped into the driver's seat of mine and off we went. The whole drive home we just talked about anything and everything. This time, that even included the future: our future.

When we arrived on campus, I told Chad to just park at my dorm. I didn't have a lot, but it was only Saturday and most people were still home for the holidays.

"You sure you don't want me to come in?" he asked, not for the first time.

"I'm just going to shower and change, unpack and then we can meet up for dinner," I offered.

"Fine. Do you want me to go park the car?" he asked.

"Nah. But you can drive it over to your house, save you some walking. I'll take it back later."

"Okay," he said, still pouting that I didn't want to go hang out at the doghouse with him. We already knew Brett and Jackson were there as they hadn't gone home for the break. I gave him one last kiss and headed inside.

I walked into my dorm room feeling great.

"Who the hell do you think you are?" Magenta asked, startling me.

I frowned. The serenity I was planning on having just flushed down the toilet. "What are you doing here? I didn't think you'd be back until tomorrow."

"Why would you think that? I didn't go anywhere."

"What? You were making that big to-do about meeting your family at Disneyland and all."

Her face flushed, and she shrugged. "I don't have to explain myself to you, freak."

I stopped and glared at her. "It was all bullshit wasn't it?"

I could see the trapped look in her eyes as she tried to come up with an excuse.

"Don't waste your few remaining blood cells thinking up an explanation, because I really don't care."

"You're such a bitch, Ember. I mean who do you think you are? You're a nobody. You hear that? A nobody! And you will not talk to me like that," she said as she hauled off and slapped me across the face.

It stung, and tears sprang to my eyes as my cheek started to heat. I was so stunned I just stood there.

"You're going to get what's coming to you. I warned you to watch your back. No one's here to protect you now. Of course I doubt anyone will even miss you when you're gone."

I was seeing red and fighting back the urge to shift. Magenta must have sensed it because she started to change right before my eyes. I didn't even know what her spirit animal was, but as sharp pointy teeth emerged and her face began to elongate, I knew I needed to get out there. Whatever she was with those deadly teeth, was no match for my tiny squirrel.

Dark green bumps started breaking out across her skin.

"You've done it now, Ember," she warned. "You're dead."

Those were the last words I clearly heard before she fully shifted into an enormous seven foot alligator. Her teeth chomped at me and I screamed. I scrambled to the top of my bed, thankful for the loft style I'd chosen. I didn't know much about alligators, but judging by her short, stubby arms, I didn't think she could reach me.

Still, she reared up on her hind legs and launched up using her tail. I screamed again and jumped back away from the edge. I heard a strange noise bellow through her and I knew it was sheer anger. Why did she hate me so much? I'd never done anything to deserve this much rage.

After a few more tries I chanced a peak over the edge and saw her begin to shift back. She wasn't fully shifted, just enough to talk. It was the scariest thing I'd ever seen, and my heart was pounding in my chest.

She stared up at me in menace, but then changed her tactics. "So, who'd you steal those clothes from Ember? You know they're knock-offs, right?"

I snorted. "No, they're not. Not that it's any of your business." I wanted to kick myself for responding. I knew she was baiting me.

"So what? You're suddenly some rich chick or something? Is this the whole new "I got with Chad and now I'm cool" look or something? I hate to burst your bubble Ember, but he's a one and done guy. You get the same notoriety as most girls on campus. Lucky you," she said snidely.

"I've always been a rich chick, Magenta. You just have your head shoved so far up your ass that you don't notice anything or anyone but yourself. And as for Chad," I started, but was interrupted by a knock on the door.

Magenta shifted back and walked over, naked to answer it. When she opened it, Chad was standing there. I bit back a smile as relief flooded me. She slinked up to my mate and put her hand on his arm. "Hey Chad. I knew you'd come around sooner or later," she purred.

"Where's Ember?" he asked ignoring her advances.

She pouted, then turned back to me and smiled. "We're a little busy in here at the moment. Come back later. Don't worry, everything's just fine, but thanks for your concern."

She slammed the door in his face and locked it.

"He's not going to be helping you today, Ember."

"Why do you hate me so much?" I finally asked in a much too calm voice.

"Look at you. Ember Kenston. You think you hide behind the glasses and frumpy clothes, but I know exactly who you are. You have everything. Everything!" she yelled. "Everything I have I've gotten on my own. No one bought me a new car, or a college education, or a whole damn hall. I wasn't going to Disneyland for Thanksgiving, that's the kind of family shit you do, not me. I have nothing, and the one thing I wanted, you take away. You went after the one guy on campus you knew I wanted."

"You're insane. You don't know me. You've never even tried to get to know me. And Chad will never be yours!"

"Really? Emmy Kenston? Poor little Emmy who doesn't want anyone to know about her famous movie star mother? I know you Ember. You're pathetic and you're weak. Chad will forget all about you and move on to the next girl and the whole time I'll be waiting, because he's mine. And it's been a long time since my girl has truly eaten," she said out of the blue with a sly grin. "I hear chipmunk is particularly delicious." I watched as she gave in to her alligator.

We were back to where we began, only this time, Chad was pounding on the door and screaming. I could feel his anxiety through the bond, but I knew I had to stand up for myself and fight back.

I sent as much love as I could to him, hoping beyond hope he'd understand. I just couldn't bring myself to tell him I loved him when I was about to face off with Magenta and knew I might not come out of it alive. I shut down the bond between us. That only made the pounding and yelling on the other side of the door grow louder, but I blocked it out, knowing I had to concentrate fully.

First the coyote, now Magenta's alligator. I was sick and tired of being a victim. I may be small, but I was not helpless. I didn't bother to peak over the edge again. She was back to taunting me and jumping into the air. Each time she got a little closer until I could see her snout breaching the edge.

I saw red and this time I embraced the shift. One second I was huddled in the corner of my bed and the next I was covered in clothes far bigger than my little squirrel body. I followed the light, trying not to get hung up in the clothes and scurried out. Just as Magenta got her first big launch and plopped onto my bed, I slid down the side of the mattress, through the slats and jumped to the top of the dresser below.

Magenta roared that creepy noise again. I dove off the dresser and flew through the air, landing on the couch. It was something I thought Chad would do and I was grateful it worked. I looked around taking in my options, but I was too slow.

Magenta caught sight of me and leapt from my bed hitting the floor with a hard thud. I think it momentarily stunned her. *Stunned*, I thought, remembering the police grade stun gun Dad had given me at the start of the school year. He had made me promise to carry it on me at all times, so I kept it in my backpack.

I looked around, then quickly back at Magenta. I was afraid to take my eyes off her for too long. I tried to judge the distance between her enormous mouth chomping at me, and my backpack. If I could just reach it.

I faked to the left and she followed. I climbed to the back of the couch and she continued to snap her jaws in my direction and began hissing. I counted to three, then scurried to my right as fast I could across the back of the couch. I jumped through the air, landing on her desk chair and propelling myself through the air. I tried to wave my tiny arms to slow my momentum, but I hit with a smack, hard against my backpack.

I was temporarily dazed as I tried to shake off the impact. Magenta couldn't move as quickly and it appeared to be difficult for her to turn around in the small space she'd found herself in. I used that time to my benefit.

The Taser didn't appear to weigh anything in my human form, but for my ground squirrel it was like lifting a car. I was fumbling and preoccupied as it popped out and went sliding across the floor.

I jumped down to retrieve it, but Magenta had gotten free and was upon me once again. I could feel her hot breath. She lunged for me and I jumped, landing easily on the top of her head. She hissed and thrashed. I grabbed hold of her eyelid and tried to hold my position. I could tell I was simply pissing her off more.

Her head swung back and forth. I watched it in relation to the stun gun. I knew I only had one chance to make this work. When she swung her head right, I held on and sucked in a deep breath. Then as she swung left I let go and went flying off. I skidded across the floor and quickly scrambled for the Taser.

Magenta went in for the kill and I jumped on the trigger, pulling with all my might. The electrodes darted out just as her mouth opened and imbedded onto her tongue. The piercing noise that followed made me want to throw up.

I ran to the door, shifting to human form at the last second and unlocking it. I came to a screeching halt. Chad was there with four rabid looking wolves behind him.

"Watch out," I yelled, as I pushed Chad out of the way and shifted in mid-air to lunge at the wolves. No one was going to hurt my mate.

Chad grabbed me with both hands and I scurried up his arm and was ready to dive bomb the wolves. When I went to leap, Chad grabbed me again.

"Ember, stop. Calm down. They're on our side. It's Damon, Karis, Brett, and Jackson."

I took a closer look and noticed one of them was a coyote, and not a wolf. I could have lived the rest of my life without seeing him in his fur after the incident in the woods. I raised my fist and shook it at them all as I vented off the last of my frustrations. I ran up Chad's arm to sit on his shoulder to be more impactful, but he only laughed.

"Stop that Ember, it tickles."

I stilled as I opened the connection between us once again. A flood of emotions filled our bond as I tried to explain what happened. My entire body shook from the shock of it all.

Chad turned and saw Magenta lying naked on the floor, looking scared, and still more than a little pissed. The electrodes were still in her mouth. The four canines growled as she moved towards us, and then she backed up quickly.

Campus police had already been called and finally made an appearance. I shifted back when I knew it was finally safe to do so. Chad retrieved a blanket from my room and covered me with it. I couldn't stop trembling as I gave my statement.

They had to call in medical to remove the Taser and take her statement. I wasn't feeling the least bit guilty about it. She'd tried to eat me, all for a boy that didn't even belong to her.

After they allowed her to put a shirt and pants on, they cuffed her and started to escort her out when she had the audacity to approach Chad.

I stalked towards her slowly. "I won't go so easy on you, if you ever lay a hand on my mate again."

Without a word she turned and stormed out of the room nearly tripping over her own two feet and dragging the poor cops behind her. I could smell the fear wafting off her.

I took a deep, calming breath, trying to regain some semblance of control.

Chad laughed. "My girl's feeling a little possessive today," he said proudly as he wrapped his arms around my waist and kissed me hard.

I started to relax and pulled away. "What are you doing here? I thought I told you to go home."

He shrugged and grinned. "I missed you."

I laughed. "You missed me? That's like the lamest excuse ever."

He shrugged, completely unaffected. "You were cursing Magenta's name pretty loudly. I just needed to know you were okay, and then she locked me out and you shut down the bond and I was freaking out."

"Is that like some mating thing?"

"What, that psycho act you just pulled on her?"

I smacked him playfully without malice. "I'm being serious."

"Possessiveness is definitely a trait of mating. Males get it a whole lot worse than females, but I dare say Magenta may argue a case for mating females everywhere after that."

The others had all shifted back to human form.

"I can't believe you tased her in the mouth," Damon said.

"That was pretty badass!" Jackson praised.

"Why'd she do it?" Karis asked. "What's her deal?"

"She fancied herself in love with Chad," I told them honestly. "She was jealous. I guess that really does turn some people into the green monster."

"Remind me never to look your way, Chad. Her psycho squirrel had my coyote cowering," Brett added.

"Don't tease, I don't even know what came over me."

Chad frowned. "You were being protective and territorial. Those emotions only get stronger and harder to control the closer we get," he said seriously.

"You mean until we seal the bond?" I asked.

He nodded. "I'm not pushing you, I'm just giving you a heads up."

"We're going to go and let you two talk," Damon said, as he clapped Chad on the shoulders.

"Thanks for having my back, guys. I don't know what I'd have done without you all here."

As they left Chad asked if I wanted to go back to the doghouse. I told him I didn't. I had just fought for my life in this room. I had stood up for myself and I was proud of that. That room was mine. I wanted to toss all her stuff into the hallway, but I refused to leave. I had conquered my fears and I was ready to reclaim my life.

I took his hand and shut the door behind us as we walked into the room.

"Someday you're going to have to tell me your side of this story, but I need to calm down first. Is it always this hard for you too?" I asked.

He shrugged understanding what I was asking. "Being around unmated males, even my brothers, won't be my favorite moments in life, but I'm controlling it. I honestly don't know what I'd do if one of them actually made a pass at you the way Magenta did at me."

I sighed and flopped down onto the loveseat. "Better than me I'd bet."

He sat beside me and kissed my forehead while running a hand gently across my back. "It won't last forever, and she definitely had it coming. I think that was probably more than just mating possession going on there."

I laughed. "Yeah, you're probably right there. She was going to attack me. I was just defending myself."

"Do you want to talk about it?" he asked.

"No. Not now, maybe never. You heard enough from my statement to the police."

"It was long overdue for you to stand up to her, you know?"

"Yeah, it was," I conceded.

"I was on my way back over here when I felt your distress and started freaking out. Want to know why I was coming back here?" he asked, and I could feel nervous energy through the bond. It set my squirrel on edge again.

"I don't know. Do I? I'm getting a bad feeling about this," I admitted. "I'm not sure how much more I can handle today."

He laughed which seemed to calm his nerves a little. He turned me to look at him. I struggled to meet his eyes at first, but when I finally did I didn't see anything bad, only love.

"I forgot to tell you something before I dropped you off."

"And you couldn't have just told me through the bond, or picked up the phone like a normal person?" I rambled, still a little nervous about whatever it was he was about to say, but enjoying the normal banter after everything that had happened.

"Nope, has to be in person. But now you're making me feel like an idiot, so I'm going to just go home and try again next time."

He stood and started to leave. My head was whirling in confusion. "What? You're serious? Get back over here and tell me whatever you came to say."

"No, it can wait 'til later."

My imagination was coming up with every possible worst-case scenario and he was just going to leave?

I got up and grabbed his arm to spin him around to me before he really left.

He grinned down at me and kissed me. *I love you, Ember.*

I froze and pulled back to stare at him. "You what?"

His nerves were suddenly back again. "I love you. I am in love with you. I'm completely crazy about you. Is that really so hard to believe?"

"That's it?" I asked.

"That's it? That's a pretty damn big *it* by my standards."

"No, I mean, there's nothing else? Nothing bad?" I needed clarification of that because he'd been acting so weird and I was expecting the worst. Plus, my nerves were still on edge after the Magenta altercation.

"I hope not, because I love you, and that would really suck if you found that to be a bad thing," he said awkwardly.

I stared at him, feeling relieved. "You had to say it through the bond first?"

"I told you I needed to tell you in person, but well, you sort of had my lips busy at that moment."

I sighed and pulled him down to kiss me again. *I love you, too.*

Ember

Epilogue

Life at the ARC was pretty close to perfect after Magenta was taken away. I was there when they came for her and recognized several of the men. Verndari. I knew enough now to understand what they meant, but I couldn't find it in my heart to care.

Dad had confessed to Dean Shannahan that Chad and I had mated and would soon be bonded. As a result, he took my room off the availability list and I was free to stay there, sans roommate for the remainder of my time at the ARC. This gave us the best of both worlds. Chad still had his bed at the doghouse, but he spent most of his nights in Kenston Hall with me. We didn't even need to apply for mated housing because I didn't have a roommate to complain about him staying over all the time.

* * * * *

I walked out of my last final for the semester. It had been a long, crazy week. I stretched and then my hand went to the bond mark on my neck. I grinned remembering how it got there, in a stressed-out frenzy in the library where we'd first met and were supposed to be studying for finals. Too bad I already had a dorm named after me, or I'd demand they rename that library in our honor instead.

"Hey, are you ready for winter break?" Melissa asked as she exited her class across the hall.

"Definitely! That was my last final. Chad should be out of his soon too."

"I still have two more tomorrow," she pouted. "Have a great vacation if I don't see you before you leave.

I hugged her. "Thanks Melissa. You too. Hey, my mom should be here soon. Do you want to meet her?"

"Maybe next time, unless you need me there for support. I'm exhausted and hoping to take a nap before hitting the books again."

I hugged her again. "Merry Christmas, Melissa. See you next year!"

She waved as she walked away.

I had broken down and told her about my mother days earlier, and she had taken it really well. I knew I didn't need to worry about her when she was more concerned about me than who my parents were. Moments like this just confirmed to me that she really was a true friend.

Chad tried to sneak up and surprise me from behind, but I'd know his scent and touch anywhere and sighed back against him when his arms wrapped around me. He leaned down and kissed the bond mark he'd left on me.

"Are they here yet?" he asked.

I shook my head. "Nope. You'll know it when they arrive."

"You really told them to meet us here in the quad over lunch break?"

"Yup. If we're doing this, we're doing it right—Hollywood style."

As if on cue, a sleek black limo pulled up between the two closest buildings. By the time the chauffeur got out and walked around to open the door, a small crowd began to form. There were gasps and a few shrieks when Alicia Kenston stepped out and gave a wave to her growing audience. Word travelled fast across the campus as Chad just grinned and shook his head.

"Well, come on. When she does something she really goes all in, huh?"

I laughed. "You have no idea!"

He took my hand as we weaved through the crowd. Mom squealed at our approach. "There's my baby girl," she said proudly as we pushed through the last few rows of people to reach her. She was fighting back tears when I hugged her.

The crowd stilled in shock. Dad shook hands with Chad, and when mom let go of me she hugged him and then checked him over thoroughly to make certain he'd survived finals week.

"Are you hungry? We can head to the cafeteria," I said just loud enough for those nearby to hear me. There was a flutter of excitement and several people quickly dispersed. "I still need to get my stuff from the dorm too," I reminded them.

"Yeah, mine's at the doghouse. The brothers are holding it hostage to ensure they get to meet you," Chad said, and while it sounded like a joke, I knew it really wasn't.

Mom looked flattered. We headed for the Café.

"I thought you said we were going to the cafeteria," Chad leaned down to whisper.

"Do you think I'm a complete moron? Everyone is taking off for the cafeteria now," I said.

The realization on his face was almost comical.

We got our food in record time. One of the cashiers even commented on how slow it had suddenly become and wondered what was going on.

"Rumor has it we're eating in the cafeteria," Mom told her.

The look on her face when she realized who was speaking was priceless. I didn't know the girl's name, but she was in two of my classes. She smiled when Mom and I put down our hot tea.

"Is this your mom, Ember?" she asked. I was surprised she knew my name.

"Yes, she is," I said proudly.

"I guess that's where you get your love of tea, huh? Ember comes in at least four times a day every day to refill her hot tea," the girl said. The nametag she was wearing said "Stacey".

"Wow, you noticed that?"

She shrugged. "I just made manager here. I make it my business to know what people are actually ordering. They wanted to take the tea off the line and I said no way because I know the other places on campus don't sell it and you're a regular around here."

Chad laughed. "See, even when you try to go unnoticed, it just doesn't work."

After ringing us up, she said, "Have a very Merry Christmas Mrs. Kenston."

Mom wrapped one arm around me and the other around Chad. "With my babies home, how can I not?"

I blushed. While we hadn't exactly been discreet about our relationship, there hadn't been some epic announcement around campus either like when Chase and Jenna mated or even Damon and Karis. I had no idea who they were but even I heard the excitement at the time.

Chad shrugged, "It was bound to leak out eventually."

"What?" Mom asked.

"That wasn't just common knowledge, Mom," I said, shaking my head and nudging her to move on.

"He marked you. I'm sure that hasn't gone unnoticed."

I could tell by the excitement on Stacey's face that she was more excited to spread that bit of gossip than brag about meeting Mom.

"I'm sure it won't for much longer now," Chad said. I knew he didn't really care. He'd be just as happy to scream it from the rooftops.

Somehow the remainder of lunch was relatively calm. If she hadn't shown up in a limo, drawing immediate attention, I don't know that she would even have caused a scene.

Dad stayed relatively quiet, just observing. I knew he was in awe knowing he was surrounded by so many shifters.

After lunch I gave them a quick tour around campus. We stopped by the doghouse and took some pictures with the brothers. I was certain my mother was going to end up on their wall before I returned from Christmas break. I wasn't really sure how I felt about that.

Mom thanked them all for watching out for me before we walked over to my dorm. Dad smiled proudly at the new Kenston Hall sign hanging over the entrance. We didn't stay long, just long enough for them to look around and grab my two packed bags. I made fun of Chad as he easily packed twice as much as I had.

Dad called for the limo and we were soon on our way. I was looking forward to our holiday plans. I had always loved Christmas. I wanted a nice, relaxing break. I dozed most of the ride home.

Ember, sweetheart, wake up, we're home, Chad said sweetly.

I groaned as I opened my eyes. My mouth felt sticky and I quickly realized the toll finals had taken on me. All I had to do was get to my bedroom and I could fall back into blissful sleep. I stepped out of the limo and stretched. I looked around, confused. There were a lot of cars parked in our driveway.

"What's going on?" I asked.

"Oh, we just have a few guests over to kick off the holidays," Mom said excitedly.

"Mom," I whined. "Did it have to be tonight? I just want to sleep for the next week."

"Take her up the servant's entrance and get her presentable," Dad told Chad.

I saw him give a conspiratorial grin as I was ushered around to the side of the house and upstairs. I feigned ignorance and let Chad lead the way. He surprised me by walking straight to our room. Normally he got turned around and confused in the house, and I was certain he'd never been to that section before.

"Come on. It'll be fun. Your mom already set out an outfit and there's help waiting," Chad said.

Whatever they were up to felt important, so I sucked it up and played along. When we got to my bedroom, Carolyn was waiting for me.

"Ember!" she squealed as she rushed to hug me.

"Carolyn! What are you doing here?"

"I'm here to get you ready for the party," she said proudly.

Just like the whirlwind I'd witnessed her conjure in the stores on Rodeo Drive, she barked commands leaving no room for arguments.

Chad was busy unpacking and disappeared into the closet. I had asked Mom to clear out a section for him to leave stuff there. When I walked in, he was cramming things into bins and shutting them quickly.

"What are you doing?"

"Nothing," he said, a little too quickly. "Just unpacking."

He tried to distract me with a kiss when I approached him, but I got by him and opened the first bin he seemed most protective of. Small bags of chips fell to the floor. He quickly picked them up and hugged them to his chest.

I hadn't spent a lot of time in his room since there was always someone around at the doghouse and we had mine all to ourselves, but his brothers had warned me about his chip hoarding. I didn't say a word, just opened the bin a little further as he shoved them back in.

"All moved in?" I asked happily.

He hung his head and gave me a sheepish look. "I am now."

I leaned in to kiss him, but we were interrupted.

"Don't you dare mess up her makeup," Carolyn screeched. "And Chad, get dressed. You're running late. Let's go."

"The drill sergeant has spoken," he sighed.

"Is all this really necessary?" I asked.

"Yes!" Carolyn insisted. "Now come on."

Chad was dressed and ready in record time. Carolyn was just zipping up my dress when he stepped out of the closet looking very handsome in a full tuxedo. My breath caught in my chest at the sight.

Carolyn did one last check over me and announced we were ready. Chad took my arm as he escorted me downstairs.

I froze at the top of the stairs as I looked around and saw just how many people were present. When my eyes crossed over a group of Chad's siblings, I relaxed and gave them a little wave.

We mingled as we made our way around the room. There was a strange variety of people there. Some were Verndari, several Hollywood actors and producers, a few of my old friends, and Chad's entire family. I mean entire family, some of which I hadn't even met previously. Not just his parents and siblings, but aunts, uncles, and cousins too. Even Jenna and Karis with all of Chad's fraternity brothers were there.

"What are you guys doing here?" I asked Jenna as she hugged me.

"Are you kidding? We weren't about to turn down a party invite at Alicia Kenston's home."

I rolled my eyes.

"You look beautiful, Ember," Karis said.

Our parents were huddled together near the big Christmas tree as Chad weaved us around the room to end up there.

Chad held my left hand as Dad clinked his champagne glass to quiet the room. I expected him to give a speech, but the room stayed quiet with all eyes on me. I started to squirm, feeling uncomfortable by the sudden attention.

Chad squeezed my hand for reassurance and cleared his throat. I turned to find him down on one knee.

"I know how much you hate being thrown in the spotlight, so for your sake I'll make this short and sweet. Ember Kenston, will you marry me?"

I gasped as he held out a beautiful diamond ring to me.

Is this supposed to be our engagement party or something?

Well that kind of depends on your answer right about now. Doesn't it? He pointed out. *Please don't keep me down here forever. I already feel like a fool in this monkey suit. This was all your mother's idea for show, but here inside our bond, I'm asking you for real. I love you so much and I want to spend the rest of my life with you in every way possible. Marry me, Ember.*

"Well? Are you going to answer him or not?" Christian yelled, making the room erupt in laughter.

I laughed and nodded, a tear slipped down my cheek. "Of course I'll marry you!"

"Yes!" Chad exclaimed as he jumped up and placed the ring on my finger.

With a dramatic flair, he kissed me for all to see.

"Eeew!" Cole exclaimed loudly, causing another round of laughter.

"We're really doing this?" I asked him as I looked around the room surrounded by everyone we cared the most about.

"We really are," he said.

Julie Trettel

Dear Reader,

I have to admit, I've been a little intimidated by the expectations of Chad's book! I truly hope you've enjoyed it. Chad and Ember were a lot of fun to write despite the pressure that came with the fun-loving fan favorite squirrel shifter!

If you enjoyed this book, please take a second and drop me a review.

For further information on my books, events, and life in general, I can be found online here:

Website: www.julietrettel.com

Facebook: http://www.facebook.com/authorjulietrettel

Facebook Fan Group:
https://www.facebook.com/groups/compounderspod7/

Instagram: http://www.instagram.com/julie.trettel

Twitter: http://www.twitter.com/julietrettel

Goodreads:
http://www.goodreads.com/author/show/14703924.Julie_Trettel

BookBub: https://www.bookbub.com/authors/julie-trettel

Amazon: http://www.amazon.com/Julie_Trettel/e/B018HS9GXS

Much love and thanks,
Julie Trettel

SNEAK PEEK

IN PLAIN SIGHT
Wolves of Collier Pack

By
Julie Trettel

Coming February 2019

Bran

Chapter 1

"Branimir, my beloved, rise."

I slowly stood on legs trembling from holding the kneeling position too long. "I pledge my allegiance to you Alpha," I said formally, careful to keep my eyes downcast in sovereign respect.

"I know the anger and hatred that runs deep within you. Channel that as you move forward on this most sacred mission. The Westins killed your father, your birth Alpha, and they continue to harbor the demon, Elena. Your journey will not be an easy one, but if you vow under the sacred blood oath as an unbreakable pledge to invoke the revenge of your father, you will forever live in reverence and gratitude in this world and into the next by all true Bulgarian wolves. Do you so accept?"

I didn't look around and not a single breath could be heard as they waited for my response.

"I do. I swear to enact the wishes of my Alpha or die trying."

I looked up to face my Alpha. He smiled down at me. I shuddered in his presence. Taking out a small dagger he held it up for all to see, then passed it to me. The blade stung as it cut through my calloused hand.

I returned the dagger to him and he surprised me as he twisted off the top of the blade. I watched as my blood dripped into the hidden amulet in the dagger's hilt. Securing the top, he handed it to the Pack Witch. I found it mildly ironic that he insisted on keeping a witch when he was so hellbent on killing the lost triplet, Elena, or Kelsey Westin as she now was called, for being a witch. I knew there was more to it than that, but the irony was not lost of me.

The witch said some words and I watched the amulet glow. "It is done. From this moment forward you are bound by blood to obey the wishes of your Alpha," she said at last passing the dagger back to my Alpha. He looked it over, satisfied he handed it back to me.

"Sir?"

"I know you will take good care of it, my beloved. It will guide you to my wishes. Bon voyage and safe travels."

"I will not let you down," I vowed.

The Alpha turned and left as the murmurs began throughout the room. It was done. I would be on the next flight to America and the most important mission of my life was about to begin. Nothing could get in my way.

Check out more great books by Julie Trettel!

The Compounders Series

The Compounders: Book1
DISSENSION
DISCONTENT
SEDITION

Westin Pack

One True Mate
Fighting Destiny
Forever Mine
Confusing Hearts
Can't Be Love

Collier Pack

Breathe Again
Run Free

ARC Shifters

Pack's Promise

About the Author

Julie Trettel is author of the Compounders and Westin Pack Series, a full time Systems Administrator, wife, and mother of 4 awesome kids. She resides in Richmond, VA and can often be found writing on the sidelines of a football field or swimming pool. She comes from a long line of story tellers. Writing has always been a stress reliever and escape for her to manage the crazy demands of juggling time and schedules between work and an active family of six. In her "free time," she enjoys traveling, reading, outdoor activities, and spending time with family and friends.

Visit

www.JulieTrettel.com

Made in the USA
Las Vegas, NV
27 April 2022

48096451R10115